Dear Azriel,

Thank you so
much! Hope you
enjoy—

Always!

Andi Jaxon

Charming

A *Charming* Book One
By. Andi Lawrencovna

First Edition:
> ISBN-13: 978-1511715430
> ISBN-10: 151171543X
> BISAC: Fiction / Fantasy / General

This is a work of fiction. The places, characters, and events portrayed in this book are products of the author's imagination or are used fictitiously. Any resemblance to actual events, locales, organizations, or real persons, living or dead, is entirely coincidental.

Works by Andi Lawrencovna

The Never Lands Saga
~ *Charming*: A *Charming* Book One ~

Coming Soon
~ *The Captain*: A *Charming* Book Two ~

Acknowledgements

I would like to take this opportunity to thank my dear friends who were kind enough to help me craft this novel. Without your encouragement and your passion, I don't know that I would have had the courage to sit down and tell the story herein.

To my family who has always supported me in my endeavors and stood behind me...even when I closed my computer screen or turned to a blank page in my notebook before they could read anything I'd written.

And to dreams, mine and yours, because dreams are what inspire us to take a leap, and oh what a leap it is.

Dedication

To anyone who has ever imagined punching Prince Charming and ended up falling in love instead.

TABLE OF CONTENTS

Author's Note

Dear Reader,

First, let me thank you for purchasing this book.

It is with great pleasure that I share it with you.

You see, a little while ago, quite by accident, I was simply sitting on the railing on my back porch, staring at the light polluted night sky, trying to find the North Star. I closed my eyes, and wished, and my railing disappeared beneath me, and suddenly the stars were the only light I could see.

It is very disconcerting to be tumbled out of your reality into someone else's. I think I might have screamed. I was certainly not dignified, not like the young man standing beside me who reached to grab my arm and stop my head long tumble over the balcony of a white marble palace to red cobblestones below. And it was a palace. It was amazing. And it was not my home in little Nowhere, Ohio where I spent way too many nights dreaming dreams about fairy tales.

My charming young rescuer smiled and settled me in a chair far enough away from the edge of the balcony that he was assured I wouldn't tumble accidentally away into nothing.

I don't admit anything, but it's possible that I wasn't sensible at the time of his rescue which may in turn be the reason why my young savior started telling me a story.

It was a very good story.

So similar to one I knew from my childhood, but not at all like it at the same time. Fairy tales are what young girls like me, or not so young girls like me, build our fantasies on. Princes and knights and magic dragons and fantastical witches filled my dreams, sparked by the Brothers Grimm or Hans Christian Anderson or folklores and nursery rhymes. And as he told me this new old story, I longed for a pen to write it down, do this retelling justice.

He refused my request.

I couldn't really blame him, especially not when his father stepped into our private interlude and asked, rather pointedly, "Who the Darkness are you?"

Well, I was going to answer, honest, but I have a rather unfortunate habit of looking up, not, as people guess, when I'm about to lie, but just when I'm nervous.

The whole meeting someone's gaze thing is beyond me.

My eyes caught on the Wishing Star, and before I had a chance to offer even my name, I was falling into the flower beds below my back porch in the middle of January, caught by a mound of snow up to my ankles without any boots on my feet or any coat on my shoulders. I managed to hang onto the blanket I'd wrapped around me, but that was it.

It was a lovely dream though.

At least that's what I thought until three weeks later when it happened again, and my lovely storyteller stared at me with a smile before lunging to keep me, once more, from falling over the side of his balcony. He offered me paper and pen this time if I would but stay to hear the end of the romance.

I couldn't refuse that.

He asked if I would return the favor, tell him a story in response, but Cinderella didn't impress him, and I had to agree that his version was better.

So, with his blessing, I took my notes home, spilled coffee on the better part of them, and began to rewrite what he'd told me.

And now I'm sharing it with you...

...at least the part that isn't stained and unreadable.

What is that old phrase? Think happy thoughts? The second star to the right? Faith, trust, and what?

Hopefully I'll have a chance to return to the Never Lands, visit my prince once more, finish the story he's been telling me in pieces.

Until then, I hope you enjoy this saga, and, remember, this is not your childhood fairy tale.

Always,

Andi

Charming

Chapter I
One
The One Hundredth Ball

ods take it, woman. Halt!"

She could barely hear his yelled order over the rushing of the wind from her galloped flight. It was easy enough escaping from the palace courtyard, making the forest road. That he chased her wasn't part of the plan, wasn't unexpected either.

She shook her head free of the thought.

"For all the hell- Stop, damnit!"

She did not obey the command hurled at her from the pounding of chasing hooves at her back.

And all this because she'd lost a blasted slipper and the bastard had decided to follow her from the ball. It wasn't enough to have danced every single waltz with the brat. No, now he was following her without a thought for himself during the middle of the night in a dark forest where bandits were rather routine and she wasn't even armed in case the wretches did show up.

A snake slithered into the moonlight cutting the path before her.

Her horse reared and her grip on its mane faltered. The folds of her gown caught around her legs, loosening her thighs' hold on the horse's flanks. When she fell, it was with little grace, arms tucked around her head to protect herself while she

Charming

tumbled to the ground, landing on her knee and rolling as quickly as she could away from the stamping hooves above her.

His horse reared in response, a motion of its owner's demands rather than being startled. While her beast bolted, he slid from his mount's saddle before rushing to her side.

"Hades—are you alright?" He reached for her, his fingers wrapping around her flailing wrists as she struggled to right herself from the ground.

"Get off of me."

She wasn't shocked that he didn't listen to her demand, continuing to help her back to her feet, even dropping to his own knee to settle her skirts around her legs more demurely.

For three days she had ridden to the courtyard of the palace, slipped easily from the back of her horse and walked with confidence through the front doors to attend the royal ball thrown for the prince to find a bride. Said prince stood now before her, his face hidden in shadow from the moonlight though the glow no doubt highlighted her own olive complexion.

This was the prince's hundredth ball.

At one hundred and thirty, he was a young man, not yet even having reached his majority. A long lived race, like her people, he wouldn't be considered an adult until his hundred and fiftieth year. He was so young to have such yearning, such shadows in his eyes.

He was handsome enough, she supposed.

Ah hell.

He was stunning. Hair black as night, eyes silver, glinting like steel freshly forged; he was a soldier trained from birth to lead and defend and it was evident in the definition of his shoulders, the way he stood before her. He loved his people, and that too was something to admire. Sharp nose, square jaw, cheekbones slightly less angular, softening his visage into something beyond classically handsome, something more charming than stately when he smiled.

Would he know a battle if he had to draw the ceremonial sword at his hip? It would be easier if this repost between them was one of steel and speed.

This was not a battle, not for him.

For her…

It was one of wits and words and hearts, damn it.

She pushed away from him, denying herself the opportunity to feel the strength of him beneath her palms a last time. Three nights were too much already. She had known better than to go to the ball, but forbidden the chance, told to stay away, she had had to.

Too dangerous, her council had said, to attempt a coup at the ball amidst all of his people. But she wasn't attempting a coup, just an assassination, which was much easier, all considered. So she'd danced with him, and it hadn't been enough to dance only the one night. Engaging him in practice in the early hours of the morning, testing his strength and his skill in a sword fight, had been an even greater pleasure for her, had been another chance to strike, another failure. Honestly, the second night of the ball should have been an end to things but he'd whisked her from the ballroom, walked with her in his gardens, spoke of his people the way she spoke of hers. She was born to fight, not talk, not dance. And yet it was the talking, the dancing she remembered most.

Not that she would think on that now.

"Why do you insist on running from me?"

"Why do you insist on chasing after?" She heard the petulance in her voice and would have blushed at the sound if she were not so well trained to hold her emotions in check.

Though she would not admit it, she enjoyed the bickering between them, the spirit he displayed. Pampered he may be, but there was a strength to him that reminded her of her people, called out to her as kin. And she could not and would not call him kin, no matter the desire swirling within her, reflected in his gaze. "I do not like you, prince. We have had our fun these past nights. Let it be enough between us."

"Never." He reached for her, pulling her close to him, bending his head to her own though his lips did not touch hers. They never touched hers, though she did not doubt he wanted to. "Never enough between us; you feel it too. I know you do."

No man's breath should smell so fresh, not after a night of champagne and wine and sweets and a jaunt through the woods. He should smell of horse and sweat and look put upon, not as though he were just now remade for the day. She must look a disgrace compared to him, her russet hair a mess around her shoulders, dress stained from her tumble from her horse.

She did not care for customs or norms, finding more comfort in breeches than the tulle of a skirt, and yet for him she had found a gown and now it was ruined and that was quite fine. She stomped her foot. Perhaps a bit more petulance, simpering condescension might make the male rethink his desire for her. "Foolish boy, I feel nothing for you." Her finger extended to poke at his chest, push him to her desires, make space between his heat that warmed her through. "You know nothing of me. Three days does not a knowledge grant. We have danced and wined but little else. If there were words spoken between us, I do not recall them."

"Liar. I was there too, my lady. We shared many words." He leaned into her finger, forcing her to retreat or bow to his advance, yield to his physicality pressing into her. "I am not blind. I know the expression in your eyes. Why run from me when you know my heart? I have told you—"

"You have spoken with the passion of a moment upon you, nothing more. Any feeling you profess is that of close encounters late at night when heads were full of drink and eyes upon the stars. What you feel is a lie, despite your words." The argument tasted of ash against her tongue. Lies upon lies and all starting the moment she was introduced at the opening of the ball and descended the stairs to the main dance floor.

She did not fall in love. Love was a thing for simpering toffs, not soldiers and assassins and princes and priests. Her people needed her return. No doubt they were already searching after her leaving.

Yet she stared at him, waiting for his words to deny her denial. Curse him.

Damn her.

"Why are you saying this? Why are you denying us?" His hands gripped her shoulders, hauling her close once more where she had let the small space between them build. "You spoke the words back to me, Ella."

"That is not my name."

He stared at her and her heart ached at the pain in his gaze. Damn him, she should not feel for him and his integrity, his humor, his compassion. This prince who was barely a man and had stolen her thoughts for three days' time and would steal her from the world she could not leave behind. No, and that was worse, that he wanted to keep her with him and she was weak enough to desire it. If he learned her name, he would hate her, hate who and what she was and yet she wanted nothing more than to tell him and see what response he would have.

Her fingers spread over the crisp feel of his doublet, the velvet brocade stitched with golden thread to set off the deep red umber, pressing for the beat of his heart beneath her hand. He'd met her at the bottom of the stairs and extended his hand. She was a silly girl, Sweet Darkness, was it really only two nights past, to not know the man who stood before her was a prince, to ignore the tittering around her when she obliged her partner and slid gracefully into a quadrille struck by the orchestra.

"Another lie." He cupped her cheek, and even knowing the road was clear at her back, that she was free to run if she but turned away, she could not move, denied the desire to, holding his gaze which so easily captured hers.

She was soft towards him.

She should not yield.

It would be so easy to take the sword at his hip and finish what her people had long sought but been denied. Who would have thought to enchant the prince in a dance? It was trickery and not the way of the woods that were subtle and swift.

"What is your name then, if not that which you have so easily said to me these past nights?"

The name was there on her tongue, waiting to sound in the air between them, hiding for a desperate moment more.

Leaves shivered with the breeze, broke across the moonlight filtering through their canopy, showing his face within the darkness. He didn't think her name would matter. Surely an Abigail or a Tabitha or even a Rebecca would not change his mind towards her? But her name was none of those. Her name was a title, and he would loathe the title once he heard it.

To have his hatred felt a worse fate than to slip a knife between his ribs and end him quickly.

"Please do not ask this of me." It was the only plea she had ever made in her life, would ever make in her life. Yes, she'd started the damn conversation, opened herself to the questioning, but she didn't want to answer him. She wasn't ashamed of who she was. But there was a niggling prayer deep in her gut, a wish to the Night to let her carry on the charade of these three days rather than go back to what she was. "Stop this." If he heard the emotion in her voice, perhaps he would take it to heart and leave her be before she was required to spout harsher realities to him. Let this memory be sweet. Do not taint it with the truth.

"I am your prince."

She looked away, fingers digging into his jacket. Her words came out a shrill laugh. "You are nothing to me."

He could not be.

She wanted to tell him to look at where he was. Ask him why he thought a noble woman would run to the forest when not a single city dweller dared venture so close to the wood's edge without a full contingent of soldiers to guard them? Had he not realized where they were, where she led them?

Her voice hardened into a growl, casting aside the airy lightness his courtiers so easily used, the lilting accent that each word rang with, to allow him a glimpse of who she was, why he should run. Her people's tongue was harsher than his, the tone distinguishable. "You are a spoiled brat barely out of his leading strings. An infant thinking himself in love. It is easy enough to spout silken promises that innocents will believe. Why would I want a whelp when I could have a wolf of the forest to wed?"

He jerked away from her, the venom of her words.

A lifetime of animosity built between their peoples, an animosity she had never herself felt, and yet could imitate without trial, sounded in her words. "A city dweller, protected by his walls." She spit on the ground separating them. He stepped back another foot to avoid the assault. "You are weak; your people are weak. Your king is an old man and his son an imbecile who is easy to tempt, too trusting by far, a walking corpse without the sense to die like prophecy demands."

Anger sparked in his eyes, the mounting fury giving his softer edges the strength of steel, unyielding, unbending. Sweet Darkness, but this was no boy before her. She knew that but couldn't help tempting him, watching the spark of temper rise. How many times had she seen the same strength enter his face, straighten his spine on the dance floor, surrounded by simpering idiots who spoke thinking their prince was a simpleton and wouldn't listen to their words?

She watched his anger flare.

He would push her away now, cast her aside as he should.

His jaw clenched tightly closed and he said nothing.

"Would you deny the truth of my words, boy?"

He snorted, a sound undignified from the man she'd come to know so well these past nights. If he smiled, she rarely saw it, and if his lips did turn up, the emotion did not reach his eyes. His face was as much a show for the world as the gown swirling around her ankles, making her a woman in his eyes rather than the warrior she was and could not change from. He would hate her when he learned who she was, an enemy on his doorstep, taken into his confidence. She'd grown on mother's milk tainted with stories of how this prince was his father's despair, a boy marked by the gods yet worshipped by none, the death of his country if he would but lay down and die.

"I am no boy."

No, he was not.

Her lungs froze when he wrapped her in his arms once more. She gripped his elbows to steady the unseemly trembling in her limbs.

She was an assassin. He should not have this power to overwhelm her the way he did.

"Tell me you do not love me."

"I do not love you." There was no conviction to her words.

"Say it again, for I do not believe you."

"Foolish boy," was barely a breath of air between them, meant more for her than him.

He bent his head to her, and she nearly gave into the desire, nearly let his lips touch hers, brand her in a way she dared not know, that he most certainly was not meant to know. She was a core of iron. There was no love inside her. She closed her eyes, blocking her mind from the thought of the sweetness of his lips, the longing to reciprocate. He pulled back without touching her, pulled back to stare into her gaze, saved her from reaching out herself.

"There is no other who compares to you." He cupped her cheek in one hand, brushing his thumb across her mouth, his expression a mix of awe and consternation. She knew that look, imagined it similar to the one on her own face. "Is it that you run from me? Is it the chase that goads me so?"

"Yes."

He smiled. "Lying again."

Truly she wasn't. That she ran from him, rebuffed him, wanted him, was part of the appeal. Merciful Night, if she'd just remained at his side until the last chime of midnight and told him no, she would be free.

Her fingers smoothed over the rumple of his sleeve.

"Tell me what it is about you that I cannot resist." He caught her stare, this prince cursed by his gods, feared by his people for the destruction his death foretold, desired for his place beside a throne. "Tell me it is a spell or a curse that you have cast upon me and I will let you go." The spell was not of her making. His eyes dropped to her lips when she made to respond that she knew darker magics than a simple enchantment of a heart. "Tell me, and make me believe, that you feel nothing for me."

She could not make the lie sound in her own head. How could she convince him that she felt nothing beyond what any of his nobles felt, was nothing but another lass out to bed a prince when she was meant to kill him, and found herself equally enthralled? She could not love a man like this. And she could not lie convincingly enough that she didn't.

Very well.

She released her hold on his arms, trailed her hands over his chest to his hips, her right hand settling over the hilt of his sword, the filigreed steel fitting neatly in her grasp. "Do you know how easy it would be to kill you, Prince?"

His eyebrows rose, questioning her meaning, her intent.

She slapped the hilt against his side, forced the scabbard to sway against the length of his leg. "Is this truly the first you've worried about it? You rode out here with no guard at your back, no weapons in your hands. The sword at your hip is for ceremony and you've no dagger to block with. It would be so easy to steal your blade and run you through. A thousand and one dreams of your death would be easily accomplished and you look at me as though I am innocent in my thoughts and deeds. You're a fool to think I could feel aught for you."

She watched the doubt tighten his eyes as he stared at her. What type of woman would speak so forthright about death or the dealing of it? "You would not harm me." She heard the hesitation, the question of his next words. "You, a woman, could not do so even if you tried. What do you know of sword and shield?" He removed his hand from her face, covering hers atop his sword hilt. "Why are you running from me? Why are you pushing me away?"

Because you cannot love me, Prince. Not and know who I am. And I cannot love you.

And love was not a thing of three night's invention, no matter what fairy tales the children told.

She could not say that though. He would take hope like a bone, bury the feeling deep within his chest so he could dig it out some day like a dog. Hope would only hurt him more when she denied it again and slit his throat.

So why couldn't she say the words to him? Why couldn't she kill him like she should? "I have no desire to be a princess."

"I have no desire to be prince." He shrugged off her words, his fingers tracing whorls over hers beneath his grip on his sword.

"You don't understand, city-man. I have no desire to be a princess. No *Dienobolos* would."

She felt the stutter of his heart despite the distance between them.

His gaze sharpened on the angular planes of her face, her leaner build compared to his people's stauncher heights. Her hair was uncommon to the city, but norm enough within the trees. The olive of her skin was more suited to hiding within branches than working ploughed fields.

He shook his head, and his hand clenched hers, the threat of danger pulsing from him in waves. "A child of the Woods would not come to the Capital. Not for any call. Not even for a chance at killing me. They would have tried it before now if they dared."

The last assassin king had forbade the attempt.

But she was queen, and her word was now law, even when council spoke in opposition.

She buried the tears beneath a growl. "Then ask me my name, prince, and hear my answer."

Darkness, but he had not pulled away from her, and she wanted him closer for a moment longer, just a moment longer before reality returned, reality that she had ignored for the past three nights of bliss at his side.

"Gaindi ni prolestul, Elichi?"

She had not heard her peoples approach, had not thought them daring enough to risk the roads this near the morning, this near the end of the ball and the emergence of the partiers on their way home. Even drunk, the city folk outnumbered her people and were equally vicious. But she had not expected to find her brethren so near the road, had not expected them to be looking for her.

His gaze snapped from hers to the tree line and she turned her head to look at the group of warriors emerging from the woods.

"There's nothing here for you, Beracsh. We're not to leave the woods—"

"And yet here you are, Elichisolos. And I see much worth my while."

Her hand tightened on the prince's sword as the leader of her mother's guard, the Priestosolos' guard, the High Priestess' guard, stepped onto the path and clear of the last row of leaves protecting the forest dwellers. The three men with him spread out at his back, seeking to ring her and the prince in the middle of the road.

"Stay behind me."

She looked quickly to the man at her side, the way he stepped in front of her, dismissing her hand on his sword to draw the blade in her defense. Had he not heard the name Beracsh gave her? Did he now know who she was? What she was? Did he really think that just because he was a woman she could not hold the title of Assassin Queen? Mistress of the Final Midnight?

He, they would kill without issue.

She, they could not come through when she fought.

He pushed her away from him, never taking his eyes from the priest who pulled two knives from his belt and advanced.

"We kill him now."

The sound of hooves rang in the distance, too far away to depend on. Her brethren wouldn't care. The sacrifice of their lives for the life of the male before her would be worth it in their minds, should be worth it in hers but still she hesitated. With the prince dead, his kingdom would fall. His father was an old man, easy enough to strike a mourning king from this world. But she did not strike at his back, turned instead to face her brethren in his defense.

Demetes smiled when she looked at him.

She would not let this prince who was honorable despite his title, wise despite his youth, die to treachery she herself had brought about. Her stupidity had led to this. She put him in harm's way when she allowed them to stop so near the threat of her people. She would not let him die for her mistake.

Her lips curled in a sneer.

Beracsh laughed behind her, his knives hissing through the air met with the cold ring of the prince's sword.

She struck too.

Elichi waited for Demetes to draw close, using the speed with which he attacked to pull him around her, taking his blade for herself before pinching the vein on the side of his throat and letting him drop to the ground.

Trao grabbed her from behind, knocking her liberated sword from her grip. The man was a master of hand to hand, had taught her all that she knew of the same, and she'd learned her lessons well. She struggled against him, drawing him closer to her, fighting to keep his attention pinned to her flailing arms and legs and away from the final man's stalking approach. He would lunge, thinking her an easy prize, but she would not die.

"You would betray your Mother for this boy?"

The Pristosolos, who had given Elichi to soldiers to raise at birth? She would that her answer could be anything but yes, but she there was no love lost between mother and child.

Her mother was the High Priest of the Darkness, and Elichi was Its sword. They did not always see in tandem. In this, apparently, they would be at odds.

But the Darkness that sang within her veins made no complaint at Elichi's actions to save the prince. She could claim it was no betrayal, even knowing that her disavowal would not mitigate her guilt.

"He is no boy."

Her weight went slack in her captor's grasp, dropping her to her knees and bending him over her at the waist. She flipped him, throwing him at the man who was too close to stop his approach, whose sword was too high to lower without damage. Trao fell on the blade, tackling the other male in the process. She retrieved her sword, slipping the sharpened steel through the leather breastplate her once weapons master wore, through his chest and out his back and into the body beneath him. They both died, the young one with a scream of pain, dishonoring the Darkness that his service was dedicated to.

The cry drew the prince's attention from Beracsh, turning him towards her in a moment of inattention, allowing his attacker to raise a knife to strike.

The dead one's scream did not pull her gaze from the battle.

Her sword flew through the air, tumbling end over end.

She watched her uncle's knees buckle, the hilt of her blade clutched by one bloody hand where it sprouted from his chest. His gaze sought hers, and she honored him by meeting it.

"Si onemi galastis, die aran." You learned well, little fox.

The prince turned his gaze to the dead man at his back, to her. Back and forth he looked until he was certain all the men were downed and she was safe, he was safe. She watched his stare rake over her fallen brethren, saw the question of her betrayal flare in his eyes.

The ground shook around them.

His guards rode to a halt.

She refused to look away from his eyes when he turned his gray metal glare to her.

"Your Highness?"

Prince Christophe de L'Avigne.

The Prince of the Walled City.

The Prince of the Ball.

And she saved him, this prince who prophecy said must die for her forest to thrive, spared by the hand of the deadliest elf to walk the land.

She bowed her head. "Your highness."

Two

The general dismounted, drawing his sword, she assumed, for a precaution against future attack, only then looking at her, down at the blood staining her hands and gown and the prince standing pristine in his doublet. The soldier advanced, and she scanned the earth for the discarded weapons of their dead foes, her dead kin. She didn't need them, but one unarmed assassin against one armed guard was different than one unarmed assassin against a cohort of armed soldiers.

"She's not the enemy, Marius."

The towering giant of a man froze though his gaze remained on her. Smart soldier, to know the true threat and not dismiss it despite her lack of a cock.

"Then what is she, sir?"

"Your new Captain, General."

The prince's words succeeded in breaking the stalemate between her and the soldier's stare, drawing their gazes to the man who they both, apparently, now served.

"You would make a woman Captain, Highness? An elf?"

That her sex was the first issue he named amused her. To think, so burly a man afraid that she was to lead part of his guard. Or was it that he was afraid he would have to fight her? She was the more vicious of the two, of that she was sure. Unpredictable. Besides, elves were known warriors, even the gatherers within the woods knew how to kill a man.

"No, Marius, *this* woman, this elf."

The prince held her gaze. She couldn't look aware, unsure of what to do if she did.

He turned to his commander, dismissing her as another soldier of little import. It was so quickly done, so easily done, that his adamant avowal of deeper emotion seemed an affectation, his words the lie over hers.

She should not feel shattered by the rebuff.

Her mouth opened to respond, but what could she say? How dare he treat her as she had tried to treat him? How dare he push her away?

"Her horse fled when they attacked. See it found and returned to the city. She'll ride with me to the palace."

Unsaid was that they had much to discuss out of earshot of his men. She wondered if, perhaps, he would return to the debate from before her brethren attacked. She doubted it. That he was so easy to read even as he hid behind his name and his position meant little when she read the beginnings of hate and fear in his face.

The prince whistled and his horse answered, trotting from the tree line to paw the ground at his feet before settling on the road.

The general signaled one of his men to dismount, hand over the reins of his horse so that she could ride the beast while others searched for her lost mount. The unseated soldier held the lead for her, but neither he nor the commander nor the prince offered her a hand to mount, not that she expected otherwise.

It had been hard enough mounting from the palace courtyard in her dress. She wasn't going to embarrass herself with the same difficulties in front of these new men.

A moment to locate her uncle's corpse, another to walk to the body and pull the sword from his chest. She passed behind the prince on her way to the blade. He flinched at her presence behind him, but didn't turn. He flinched again when the wet suck of the sword pulled from the chest cavity.

She laid the blade along the ground, letting the blood glint bright red in the rising morning sun, dirt blowing in the gentle breeze, picked up and strewn over the steel, a macabre reminder of the massacre that she perpetrated here.

She pulled a knife from rigid dead fingers, the steel more maneuverable than the sword would have been for her purposes.

With a twist of the knife, she made a slit in her skirt, the fabric parting from mid-hip to hem, baring the layers of petticoats and tulle beneath. She made the same slash on the other side. It took some effort, but she managed to cut the stays on her undergarments, let the wash of white fluff and silk slip from beneath the heavy brocade over-gown and fall unheeded to the dirt covered road. Someone hissed when she stepped from the mess and her leg showed through the seams of the fabric. Another hushed the first soldier, though the horses shuffled with their riders' unease.

Freed of the restricting gown, Elichi returned to the waiting sword, knife shoved through the waist of her gown, dangerously close to the flesh of her hip as she bent to retrieve the weapon.

She glared over her shoulder when the brute called for her to stop.

It was the prince's hand that stopped Marius' advance, letting her finish whatever it was she was about.

Careful not to disturb the blood any further, she stepped to the edge of the forest, the edge of her homeland, no more. She pressed both hands together over the hilt of the sword, raised them into the air so that the flat of the blade stood between her and the wood, a barrier she could not cross. One hundred years for each life she'd taken. One hundred years for each man of the woods who would return to the Darkness and know light no more.

She didn't hesitate in burying the blade in the earth, letting her strength carry the metal deep into the ground so that the blood would nourish the grass, a last homage to the men who once walked the forest paths. Her hands slipped past the hilt guard, palms sliding along the edge of the blade, cutting deep into her skin, letting her blood wash with her kin's.

They were not the only to die this day.

The woman she was, was no more.

She cut a lock of her hair with the knife at her waist, knotted the bright length around the hilt of the sword, and walked away.

There were words, questions from the general, from the soldiers, men unhorsed to see to the blood dripping from her clenched fists into the dust.

He wrapped her hands in the remains of her tulle skirts.

She met the prince's gaze when he pressed her fingers into her palms, forcing pressure on the wounds. "They'll heal quickly."

"They're not healed yet."

He led her to a mount, and she stepped into the stirrups without aid, settling the ripped skirt around her legs as best she could. His hand hovered over her calf, ensuring she was steady, waiting until she met his eye before mounting his own steed, the flash of emotion there and gone, a fantasy forgotten in death and blood and soldiers and steel.

"What the hell was that?" "Is she insane?" "Why would he bring an elf into our midst?"

Words circled around her, whispered though the silence of the road did not hide them from her ears. She did not respond, staring instead at the reins tied round the pommel, wondering how she would hold them with the pain in her hands.

Yes, she would heal, and heal quickly, once she had a chance to tend the wounds, but for now she didn't know how she was going to manage to ride, and yet didn't regret her actions in the slightest.

She honored her homeland, her people, and said goodbye to them. She claimed her misdeeds, accepted her exile.

Now she would live with the choice.

"With me."

The prince settled into his seat and kicked his horse into a gallop, not looking back to see if she followed or not.

Her horse decided without her insight, racing to catch its mate far ahead. She didn't need the reins, her mount trained to follow its leader without a rider's direction.

She followed after the man, knees hugging tight to the horse's withers, flying at the prince's side. His guards did not rush to join them, apparently remaining to investigate the scene, give her time to speak with the man whose life she'd saved, discuss her actions without the commander as witness, the confusion of her rituals.

The prince slowed on the coastal road, keeping to an easy trot now out of earshot of the soldiers who finally fell into line behind them.

"Elichisolos, Elichi, is not a name but a title." His gaze turned to hers, quickly back to the road. "The elves call their greatest warrior such. No other would claim the title for fear of death by the hands of the one who it belonged to."

"You know of my culture."

"The *Dienobolos*. The Children of the Woods. A myth but to any who roam too close to your boarders and learn the skill with which you hide your presence."

"Not so much a myth to you, it would seem."

"I am a prince. You declared war against my kingdom when the walls first rose. I've learned your history from the moment I could speak." His shoulders stiffened, spine straightening though he didn't look at her again. "Was it your kin who said my death would fell the walls? Would give you back the land your forests once ruled?"

"I don't know."

His was a question for the priests.

She was a soldier.

He was silent after her answer. She took the moment to study his proud face, the eyes dulled behind an emotionless mask, the man of only an hour before hidden beneath the face of the prince. This face she knew, heard stories of, remote, aloof, unyielding and yet somehow she knew he would be kind if he could. That kindness called to her; that kindness would get him killed.

Or perhaps it was not kindness that she sensed. Something more, deeper. Loyalty, honor. She'd threatened his life and the lives of his people if he died. Yet he'd spared her, claimed her despite it all.

"You cut your hands; you cut your hair. Ritual, yes? Ritual of the hunt?" He did not try to hide the suspicion in his voice.

"Of death."

A flash, only a flash of emotion in those gray eyes of his staring back at her.

"I killed my kin to save your life. I am as dead to my people as the ones who lie motionless back there." She raised her bandaged hands, the white cloth stained red as her palms seeped blood. "I accept my fate, and they will know that."

"And hunt you for it?"

She nudged her horse until it stepped closer to his, the motion subtle, unnoticed. "We hunt those the Darkness deems must die. We hunt those whose lives are bartered to the woods for something else."

"Assassins."

"You feed your people with crops in the fields. We have no fields."

He snarled, but truth was truth.

"We might be assassins; some of us might be assassins—"

"The ones who worship Echi, the Final Midnight."

That he knew her religion even that much shocked her. She blinked, hoping he did not notice the widening of her eyes. "But even the Echi has rules to follow, Kit."

He reined his horse in quickly, drawing his mount to a harsh stop, hers following his command. "Let us be very clear, elf. You will address me as 'Your Highness, Your Majesty, or Lord.' You have no right to call me by name." The flame of anger in his eyes was a harsher, crueler flame than the spark on the road before. There was true hate there now, distrust.

She ached to see it. "Apologies, your Highness."

He clicked his tongue, urging his horse forward.

She did not expect him to speak to her again.

The fresh breeze off the sea lifted her hair from her neck. The heavy strands had fallen from the delicate curls she wore for the ball. Now the mass hung heavy down her back, all but the hank she left behind at the sight of the battle. Moist air clung to her face, weighed down her eye lashes. The Elichisolos did not cry. She would not now, even when the position was dead to her.

"You're young to be your peoples' Elichisolos?"

"Elichi is fine," she hesitated, not liking the feel of 'your highness' on her tongue. So she gave him no name, ignored the inelegance of her speech to continue beyond the thought. "Does age make any difference in the taking of a life?"

Even in the light, the Dark finds ways to cast shadow.

There is no hiding from the Blackness of Night, for even the sun falls to its cover at the end of the day.

She shook her head though he was not looking at her. "I am not the Elichi any longer."

"The title is yours unto your death."

Another tenant an outsider of the woods should not know and she was unsurprised to find he did. "I am dead to the woods, my Prince."

He turned to look at her now, she saw it from the corner of her eye while she stared ahead, though he did not correct her choice of address.

"In saving your life against the threat of my people, I betrayed the greatest vow we take. I killed my brethren to save a foreigner, whose death they have long sought."

"They, but not you?"

She didn't answer. "Do you deserve to die, Prince?" She met his stare. "The Darkness has long spoken to me. I am its servant; I obey its commands. You were not meant to die by my hand, by my brethren's hands. A god may say something to one person that another will not hear. I believe myself right in my actions, as they will believe in theirs."

"You were never going to kill me?"

She could lie, tell him his life had always been safe in her hands. But it was his smile, the smile he showed her that no one else seemed to see amidst the swirl of gowns at the ball, that spared him. "Sometimes it is blind luck that we follow our god's commands when the order is yet unclear." She felt no pull to end his life now, had not felt it then upon their first meeting either, but it was her choice not to end his life, and the Darkness' allowance that kept him breathing.

They stared at each other in silence, and he did not ask if his life was safe again.

His mount sidestepped, his leg pressing to hers in the momentary brush.

She closed her eyes so he wouldn't see how very much she enjoyed the accidental touch. With her eyes closed, she wouldn't have to see if he flinched away from her, scowled and increased the distance between them, growing since the moment her people stepped from the trees.

She leaned back on her mount, laying against the saddle and the horse's spine to stare at the stars shining despite the sun's waking light. "You pray to the gods for your salvation. They are your protectors, and healers, and avengers. We do not have that in the woods. We believe in the Darkness, the Great Unifier, the Place from Which We Came and Will Return. The woods hold the heart of darkness, shade of the trees, pitch of the night. There are no stars to see through the leaves, no sunlight that is not filtered through the branches. I am a child of those shadows, cast into the light. I've betrayed the bosom that is my family and been rejected because of it, all for a man my head tells me deserves a chance at life, whose death would not be the salvation my brothers would have it." She turned her head resting on the horse's rump, uncaring of her precarious position on her mount. "Are you worth it, prince? Are you worth the destruction of my life for the safety of yours?"

"Are you truly the Elichi?"

She snorted. "If I'd wanted you dead, you would not have felt the blow, never seen my face."

He held her stare, something comforting in knowing he saw her even in the blankness of his gaze. "I don't know if I'm worth it."

She straightened, her mount shuffling beneath her. "Which perhaps makes you the most worthy of salvation." She hesitated, staring ahead at the walls beginning to peak in the distance, the palace topping the rise. "You would give me a home, within your walls, a place in your guard?"

"I would keep you close."

Close as an enemy could be kept.

He did not need to say the words for her to know their truth. What trust was between them was shattered, what love he professed buried beneath the earth with the bodies left to rot upon the road.

"I accept, Prince."

He nodded, waved a hand overhead and his soldiers rode hard to flank them, placing the prince in the center of their tight ring as they moved ever closer to the city before them.

They rode in silence, only stares passed between them, between the soldiers staring at her.

The prince never looked back.

Three

S he settled in a room off the barracks typically used as overflow servants' quarters for the ball. Now that the festivities were over, the quarters were empty and she had the run of the small three chamber area.

It took her most of the day to clear out the three other beds from her newly assigned quarters, but she wasn't going to be sharing, no matter what the guards or the prince thought of her. The front space was the living area, a kitchen and small storage box if she desired to cook her own meals. She supposed she would have to ask if meals were provided to the soldiers, or if she was on her own, but that was a thought for a later time. There was no door between the walled off kitchen and the sleeping chambers, not that the arrangement concerned her much.

The second two rooms had a thin curtain rod separating them, likely to provide privacy for those changing and those sleeping on different shifts in the palace. She pulled the thin fabric back, opening the space for herself, enlarging the room.

A bed, of course, in the middle, something bigger than the damnable cots she'd already removed. A small table that could serve as her desk, a chair or two to relax in. The small closet was big enough for her meager belongings, and her trunk could fit against the wall without notice. She'd have to find a lamp, some candles. She probably wouldn't light them often and they might be an expense she could live without.

But most humans were afraid of the dark.

She was human now, wasn't she? One of the city's own? A Tornaldian. Or did they call themselves Spinichians? She didn't want to be associated with a vegetable grown in the fields. And she couldn't call herself an elf if she wanted these people to accept her.

She pushed the thought aside, sneezed at the dust in the air blown about in her passing. There was a bathing chamber off the farthest corner, a door discreetly tucked into the wooden wall. It was a luxury she'd never known in the woods where the most she hoped for was a private pool for a bath, heated by the earth's core if she was lucky, usually frigid beneath a leafy canopy of trees. When she turned the spigot for the bath, hot water flowed out. She didn't even need to use magic to heat the stream.

If she allowed herself, she could become quite comfortable in this new world, complacent.

She was human.

She was not an elf.

Human.

Less than one day exiled from her woods, and already she missed the shadowed groves that once soothed her.

A shake of her head, a slam of the bathroom door, her fingers glancing over the familiar and yet foreign feel of wood beneath her hand, and she walked away. There was no bark to scrape at her palms, rub against her feet when she walked across the ground. Everything sanded smooth, whitewashed, falsely bright to her eyes. She missed the dark grains of maple trees, poplars, the scent of pine and majesty of oak. Without a candle, at least she wouldn't have to see how the city dwellers had banished nature from their world.

Plants.

She'd buy plants and trees that could survive in her muted prison to make it feel more like home. Ivy to cover the disfigured walls; vines to form a canopy over her bed for the night. Green blankets, not leaves, but fabric, so at least she could pretend she was surrounded by the forest even as she was so far away.

Decided, she looked once more around the room, empty now of beds and dressers and everything that didn't belong to her, empty as she had nothing of her own.

She—

Darkness, she didn't even have a name anymore. She wasn't the Elichi. She wasn't "girl" as her father named her as a child, the name she bore until she claimed the position of highest worshipper of Echi.

She had no name, no bed, no clothes but the ripped gown covering her until she retrieved her things from the inn. Nothing but a job unwillingly given and a room she'd rather set fire to than sleep within.

Easier to start with the basics. The inn where her belongings for the ball were housed. She'd gather them together, move them to her rooms, find the prince who stranded her in this hellhole and she'd think of the rest when the time came.

CR&D

Three guards ranged before her door, a quick look to one another before they bowed their heads to her presence. Accepting their accompaniment seemed intrusive to her already chaotic life. Denying their accompaniment suggested that she had some nefarious purpose. No doubt they would report the same to their general, since she doubted the prince would stick her with a spy since he was against the same himself.

She nodded at the men, unsmiling since she was their "captain," whatever that implied, and snapped her fingers for them to follow in her wake. Asking their directions would have made the trip through the city a quicker journey, but she had an empty room to return to, despair at her current situation, lack of anything resembling companionship in her future, so she took her time journeying to the inn.

When she left the lodgings, she whistled loud enough to attract the attention of her poor shadows and the general populace around her. One of her guards answered her motioned summons, and she patted him on the back, forcing him to bend over and grab the handle of her trunk while she winked at the other two uniformed men and wound her way back to the palace via the central square and the vendors whose shops closed at the advent of night. It would have been nice to have found something other than her now modified dress to wear for the next day, something suitable for a lady, but she wasn't really a lady in the human sense of the word.

She would make do with what she had brought with her from the forest.

Her mother would likely hold a bonfire someday soon, the smoke rising within the woods for the surrounding towns to wonder at. Exiled, she was no longer part of the clan, her belongings must be destroyed, all reminder of her person annulled.

Four hundred years.

Four hundred years would see her exile pardoned and her feet allowed tread on the forest paths once more. A hundred years for every life she'd taken against the Dienobolos. It was a long time, even for a person whose lifespan was nearly quadruple that. She was young enough that four hundred years was both an eternity and not long at all considering her life span. Three millennium and she was not even two hundred years into it. The elves would still consider her barely an adult by the time she could to return to their fold. And she'd lived her life for them, for all they asked of her. She'd killed and saved and sacrificed and in two hundred years, the only moment she'd taken for herself had been the one moment that stripped her from the forest for what wasn't nearly an eternity but felt damn sure close to it.

And now she had nothing.

No food, no money, no friends to acclimate the change in her circumstances with. She was as dead to those who she once knew as the men lying on the forest road.

Would she be allotted a stipend for her services in the guard?

The thought sprang to mind as she passed a seamstress' shop, the window displaying a rather florid gown that looked like it must weigh a good amount and couldn't be all that pleasant to don.

Yes, think about money, about distractions. There was no place for self-pity in her life, not before, certainly not now.

Surely the men who served the prince were paid some sort of pittance?

She could pick a few pockets. No one would know she was there. It would be easy enough to touch the Darkness in their minds and wipe the memories from their—

No, she mustn't think like that. She was not of the woods and so had no right to the magic within her soul that was so connected to her riven home. A clean break was what she must envision. It was harder than she thought it would be, starting over as nothing. And she didn't know why she'd made the choice she had, been driven by the Darkness in her heart to protect the prince even against her own hard felt beliefs.

Do not think on it.

Damnit no, think about money. About soldiers. Any-thing!

The barracks were not nearly large enough to accommodate all the guards and some of the men must be living within the town itself. That would imply they were paid for their services and that she too could insist upon some compensation.

Safe, that was a safe thought to have. Yes, the soldiers and whether they slept in the barracks or beyond the castle walls. What would she do with a stipend? She'd never truly needed money before coming to the city. Was begging to be paid in court dances and noble smiles a reasonable fee, or should she beg for coin and ignore the frown on his face?

സ്റ

Her trek through the city took her past a baker. The sign on the door listed to one side. A display window housed old baguettes, the edges greening with mold though noticeable only if one looked closely. Yeast filled the air, almond bread, if she had to guess though the old loaves had no nuts atop them. Still, the scent was enough to draw her nearer, hoping to catch a glimpse of the proprietor within the darkened shop, beg a roll or two. Shadows moved within the room, but no one came to the door at her knock.

"M'lady, there is a tavern a block down that is open late."

She turned to her escort, the men sweating, hoisting her trunk in the air. "Lead the way, gentlemen."

The pub glowed with the merry light of a fire flickering within the stone walls. Hers was not the only stomach that was grumbling.

She had enough borrowed silver on her person to treat herself to a small meal, even a glass of ale for her wayward chaperones if she tread lightly with her coin. She waited for the men to reach her, her trunk settling with a solid thump on the ground outside the tavern.

"I appreciate the aid, gentlemen. As I've not much coin yet, I can't offer you more than a pint, but I'd like to treat you to that if you're able."

The one who she initially corralled into carrying her things flashed a quick, easy smile, young to be in the guard.

She smiled back, noting the way he stood so openly faced to her, offering no protection to himself against approaching attack. She could fix that, if she proved capable of training these soldiers.

"We're allowed one a day, miss, unless we're off duty."

"And watching me is considered a duty then?"

"Yes, Miss. I mean—"

Her laugh took the man aback. To be fair, she was rather uncertain about its exuberance herself. She sounded giddy, and the knot in her stomach was anything but happiness. Best not to think too long on the sick feeling, lest it manifest into true form. Better to push it aside, and let things unfold as they ought, the dread would pass once she settled into this new life of hers. "Well then, I shall do my best not to make your time any more onerous than it already is. A pint, good sirs?"

The man who was bringing up the rear of their party nodded, eyes scanning the crowd around them, a true soldier, then. He would likely not partake of any refreshment but water. She might join him in that endeavor.

She acknowledged his austerity with a flickering glance of her own, allowing the guard to see that her flippancy was more act than not. A quick bite, and then they would leave. Already the night was nearly past and morning came early outside the woods.

She ordered a bowl of stew for herself, and a round for the men. The young one ordered his own meal, and the silent one gnawed on a hank of bread left for the table. The third one gave a yawn, and had to fight sleep to drain his tankard. He should have eaten something, but he didn't, and soon was snoring while she and her new companions finished their meal. He woke with a start when the youngster kicked out the man's chair legs. His hand went to his knife first, drawing it partially from its scabbard at his side before realizing the jest against him. She watched. Fast and precise. The prince's soldiers were not soft in their duties. This was good, and hinted that they had a chance of growing more proficient if set the right tasks. Mental notes, all of them, jotted down and forming into a plan for the morrow. She occupied herself with a list of jobs, her mind settled on the immediacy of her new job, rather than the uncertainty of what it would entail.

At the end of her meal, she nodded to the men to precede her from the pub while she waited for the owner to take payment for their meal. The elder man waved her off, and she blushed when she realized her new guards had taken care of her fare for her. She would repay the debt at some point.

They wound their way more easily now through the city, anxious to return to their rooms for whatever sleep remained in the night. She bid them fair dreams at the door to her quarters, taking her trunk to her room without further assistance. She had no bed to sleep on, no chair to rest her feet. Her hands ached from the slices across her palms but those were a passing concern.

She spent the night staring out the window, sharpening the sword hidden deep in her belongings until the edge gleamed and cut the air around her.

At the first whistle of bird song, she summoned her courage and stood to face the new dawn, so much brighter than what she knew and understood.

Four

She stood in the vestibule, watching as men in uniforms lined up in rows and squared off against their opponents. It was their version of entertainment, thin foils lending skill in developing speed for the attack. Speed and accuracy, as she watched men find marks on their opponents, some even mimicking the movement of pulling a sword free before taking the offensive once more. Still, if real battle were to come, the thin blades would do nothing against an armored opponent, and she'd not heard that the steel had any ability to stop a spell or dragon fire spit at a man.

She could not deny that it was fun to watch, something she'd not considered of her own training within the woods.

The prince paired off with the commander, both men saluting each other before beginning their dance of thrust and parry, riposte and remise.

The movements were easy enough to emulate; the forms similar to what she knew of knife fighting, requiring the same skill.

She stepped from her post at the wall, having decided she'd had enough of this pointless back and forth.

"Is that a girl?"

Her eyebrows rose at the shrill call of one of the men now pushing away the foil of a fellow's blade touching his chest. Truly, there was nothing all that different between his physique and her own. A bulge at the groin, but they both had two legs and arms. So his breasts were less defined against the cambric of his fencing jerkin. She'd bound hers down so not to get in her way while fighting.

Surely some of these men had lain with a woman before? Just because tradition dictated abstinence amongst the nobility, the lower classes found what amusements they could and a guard was very unlikely to be true nobility.

The prince spun out of an attack by the general, stopping their back and forth to look at her where she stood in the doorway to the practice area.

"What are you doing here, El-li?" He stumbled over naming her, shortening what was once her title into a strange amalgamation of the name he'd known her as at the ball and who she no longer was. She was no longer either person.

She would be "Eli." Yes, the name settled on her tongue and she found it palatable.

"Training, Sir." Eli let her gaze wander over the men ranged before her, some with skill, many lacking.

"Kit, she's a woman. She's wearing breeches."

"For the Darkness' sake." She traversed the parquet floors, ignoring the way the sun glinted off the multitude of colors in the wood and cast the room in a rosy glow. She stopped before the prince and the general and crossed her arms over her chest, knowing that their gazes glanced there with her motion. "If you cannot get over the presence of a distraction on a battlefield, how do you expect to survive a war?"

"We're not on a battlefield, Captain." The general's deep baritone settled deep in her gut, grounding her in the moment. A talent, almost like magic, if he could calm his men with just a word or two. She'd have to remember the phenomenon for the future. "This is simple sport."

No, he didn't believe that, despite the levity of his words. He didn't want her here. He didn't trust her. She wasn't sure she would act differently in his situation. Very well. "Then where am I to train?"

"In the training courtyard, beyond the barracks. We only meet there thrice a week during peace times."

She turned her gaze to the prince, the twitching of his lips into something more than just the congenial mask she remembered him gracing other maidens with during the ball. He liked her sparring with his commander, the irreverence with which she spoke. "Then why fence, if there is no point to the endeavor?"

"Stamina, Captain." The general rested his foil against his shoulder.

"Have you ever tried before?" The prince's looked quickly away from her gaze, refusing to hold her stare.

She'd fenced, but not, precisely, in the same way he was asking her. The divot where the blade had pierced her shoulder pained her on exceedingly hot days. And she didn't think he'd enjoy the knowledge of her second time with foil in hand. "I'm proficient with this weapon, if that's what you're asking."

"It's wasn't, no." He turned from her, gripped his gloved hand along the length of the blade and cleaned it of what dust had gathered there in the moment they'd been forced to converse.

Had she angered him?

She hadn't meant to.

Did he truly not want her there?

She wasn't leaving.

The Commander responded. She watched the prince's shoulders tense at the decree. "Geoff, pair with Captain Eli.

You're a novice. Go through the motions together and we'll see how you've done at the end of the bouts today."

Bouts?

And he was pairing her with a novice?

"But sir, she's a woman. I can't fight a woman."

Blunt, and amusing, she found the combination worked best when dealing with prissy little boys. "For the Night's sake. Do you think that my lack of cock will really impact whether I can use a sword or not?"

The commander blurted out a guffaw, quickly silenced to not undermine her new authority.

She found another male ogling her, most of them were. "You," she pointed to the unnamed noble, uncaring that he likely outranked her, though his age looked far younger than her one hundred and ninety-seven. "Fetch me a pair of socks, and hurry up with that."

"Socks?" The whispered question quickly made its way around the room.

The boy didn't hesitate to obey her order.

This time it was the prince's eyebrow that reached skyward.

She bundled her hair into a knot at the back of her head to keep her tresses from getting in her way, from being too obviously feminine in appearance.

Brazen balls. No woman had held the position of Elichi before she ascended to the title. For forty-seven years she'd been the best killer in her clan, in all the clans of the woodland folk. She would have lasted longer, if she'd not…abdicated…to follow Kit to the palace.

Yes, she liked that. Abdicated. It felt better than the truth. A lie to balm her wounded, lonely soul.

The boy skidded to a halt, his boots lacking traction on the wooden flooring enough to stop him without sliding forward. One pair of stockings, not socks as she'd requested. The sturdier material would have done better, but she could wind the stockings into the right shape all the same.

She took the silk and braided it into a thick rope, barely six inches long when she was finished. It didn't really matter, as it was a demonstration more than anything else. "If it's a cock you want," she pushed the bundled fabric into the tight fit of her breeches, adjusting the disguise until it looked like the appropriate appendage it was emulating.

The prince choked, bowing forward to fight for a breath free of laughter.

His movement loosened his hold on the foil in his grasp. She snatched it easily from his fingers, slowing her movements enough that the boy in front of her realized she was going to attack before she swung her arm in an overhand slash, knowing that the blade she wielded would easily be blocked and was not used for such a move. Per the rules of fencing, she should be disqualified. But that wasn't the point now, and she shifted forward when he moved to block her, spinning inside his guard and knocking her opponent back a step, snagging his dropped sword before it fell to the floor and ending with the point of the prince's blade at the young man's throat, the second sword's tip just barely touching her sock bearer's *equipment*.

"That is not fencing."

"No, but I wasn't trying to fence. Just prove a point." She pressed a nudge forward, enough to ensure that her opponents felt the press of her blades against their more vulnerable areas.

"Are you quite through?" Prince Christophe stood at her back, his bent arm just brushing against the flowing linen of her shirt.

"Will they disregard my lack of a penis to fight me?" She did not take her gaze off the two men cowering before her.

"I think we will all be quite willing to disregard that rather unique trait of yours."

She nodded. "Then let us fence." With a flip of the foils in her hands, catching onto the blunted blades and extending the pommels back to their original owners, she moved into position to train.

The prince waited to retrieve his weapon, stepping into her guard to do so. "After practice, you'll show me how you did that."

She inclined her head in agreement.

"Fetch her a blade." Voice lowered, he said to her, "And take those damn socks away."

She caught his eye, unable to resist the quick retort. "Jealous?"

His face flushed red, eyes glancing down at her displayed groin before squeezing tightly closed. "I'm not sure that's something I can—" He gulped.

She laughed. "And yet men parade about the same every day. How disappointing."

Kit didn't respond, though his cheeks grew a brighter shade of red beneath her gaze.

A man tossed her a foil and she caught the hilt, swung twice, before resting the blade on her shoulder and waiting for her prescribed partner to regain his feet from where she'd knocked him to the floor.

The prince turned back to his bout, and she parried her partner's thrust.

The boy managed a good defense, but was too timid to attack, whether because of her sex or his lack of command with his blade she didn't know. After the third such advance, she pulled the boy to a corner of the room left free of fencing men, and adjusted his grip on the hilt.

"It's a light blade, that's true, but you can't hold it like it will sting you same as your opponent's weapon."

They parried and thrust in tandem, her pupil mimicking her movements until he moved smoothly, or nearly fluidly, through the sequence. She worked with the lad well past the time the other partners stopped for a rest, her student more than willing to listen to her advice now that her skill was proven with more than just cheap thrills and tricks. They both panted with exertion by the ringing of the midday bell.

"Last bout, gents, and lady." The general called the match.

She made to salute Geoff, but was stopped before her blade rose in the motion.

"His highness would see your skill for himself, Captain."

Her gaze traveled over the general's face, noting the slight grimace with his command. If she were him, she would not want someone like her partnering the royal personage without proper vetting. She couldn't fault the soldier for his caution.

That didn't mean she would back down from the bout though.

Eli, the name settled on her though she'd only had it for an afternoon, squared off against the prince, watching Kit adjust the gauntlets on his wrists.

She'd refused to call him by name during the ball, not wanting the intimacy of it to further compel her heart to his. Did it matter now, how far she fell? She was stuck with him for the next four hundred years at least, would it not be easier to regain a part of the companionship that had existed between them a night ago rather than this stalemate between their persons?

Yes, if she managed to force the feelings simmering in her gut to friendship, then love would flee.

"*En garde.*"

He thrust and she parried.

They moved back and forth along the lines of the floor, neither forcing an attack while they tested the other's mettle. She found him to be competent, willing to hold back rather than show her his skill at the forefront of their engagement. A wise tactician, so it would appear. She followed a similar mindset, though it took her only a few moments to know that her skill outstripped his. Of course, her skill was based on ignoring the rules of engagement and creating her own, better suited to a true battlefield rather than a test in a controlled room.

She refused to lose regardless.

He scored the first hit, and she quickly followed with her own, a second and third and the match was hers. She could have taken his sword at the end; he'd left himself open to the maneuver but she was congenial, and did not divest him of his weapon before his men. His eyes narrowed at her like he knew what she'd done. She shrugged, her only acknowledgement of his belief.

"A wonderful display, your highness. And Captain, a true swordsman has entered our midst. I look forward to watching you upon the practice field with real weapons in your hand." The lie made her smile. The commander was dreading her appearance in the lists, for, with a real weapon, she was all the more likely to move to kill his prince than with a foil. Accidents tended to happen on the practice field.

Eventually, Marius would realize she was dedicated to ensuring no accidents befell the prince. She would prove it to herself as well.

The men dispersed, only the prince and his personal guardian remaining behind with her.

"You had me. You had my sword but you didn't take it."

He did not pose the remark as a question, so she did not feel the need to respond with an answer.

Before he could ask her why, she moved to his side, tossing the general her blade to mirror Kit and his stance beside her.

"General, do you remember Kit's" the prince stiffened at his nickname, "stance for the last exchange?"

The man nodded, raising her blade to mimic his lord's position.

"Good. Now, do you see…"

СЗ80

They spent another hour discussing technique, practicing the movements that she'd honed beyond an art form into a deadly dance if the blades were tipped and she were aiming to kill. She squared off against Kit, practicing with him once more. This time, when he opened himself to her attack, she took his blade and knocked him to the floor.

He went to stand only to notice that her blade was at his throat.

"That's enough for today. You're exhausted. And I'm exhausted. The longer we drill, the less you'll learn and the more likely you're to be injured."

"Or you."

She smiled at his sullen response. They both knew that if one of them was to be injured, it would not be her.

Marius returned to the room, she'd not noticed him leave, with a platter of sandwiches in his hand, a pitcher of water on the tray. "It's nearly supper already. You've been at this since midday. I thought I'd have to physically separate you if you weren't done by the time I returned." He paused to truly look at the scene before him.

She'd knocked Kit to the ground before.

This was the first time she'd pinned him with a sword too.

His voice tried for nonchalance, though his eyes hardened at the sword she had pointed at their prince. "Perhaps I'm too late."

She pulled away quickly, a final salute, before she extended a hand and helped Kit to his feet. His fingers lingered in hers a moment longer than necessary. He did not meet her gaze though, and she felt a flash of something at his denial.

"Thank you, Marius."

The general placed the tray of food on a side table and handed Kit a towel from his shoulder.

She stood there, an awkward third to their easy comradery.

She was not jealous of the exchange between them.

She wasn't.

But she missed having Kit to herself. Even in a crowded ballroom, they'd been alone together.

Stop it.

Stop thinking of that. It's over and done. No more. It will never happen again. She would damn sure not cry.

Killer. Assassin. Guard.

Lover was not a name that she claimed.

She'd given any hope of a lover up the moment she'd attained the position of Elichi. Tomal had refused her bed after she'd proven the Darkness in her heart. She'd refused Kit who was her second best bet. A lie, about being second.

Her gaze skittered to his when he sat at the small table and read the papers that had come along on the tray from his commander.

They'd not dismissed her. And yet they ignored her presence like they had.

She was not used to being unseen, at least when she was not trying.

Eli didn't like it.

Her fingers tightened on the hilts of the swords she carried. She wanted to go back to sparring. Wanted his focus on her once more. But he laughed at something the commander said, and her thoughts were too angry in her head for her to hear the man's response.

It took all of her concentration to exit the room unnoticed, to leave the two men behind without looking back and hoping they would call her to stay. She deposited the foils in a large stand with the other noble's blades piercing the wood.

She didn't care. Truly. She didn't care.

She didn't sit on the bench outside the practice room waiting for him to emerge because she cared but rather because someone had best guard him for a few days unless an assassin attack or some other such fool made to hurt him.

When he emerged, walked past her without noticing her in the shadows, it was harder to hide the hurt his lack of recognition caused her.

She followed him regardless, gritting her teeth to keep from calling out to him to turn.

Five

She watched him as he shrugged the fencing jacket off his shoulders, the thick material bunching around his wrists until he freed the cuffs and caught the coat before it fell to the floor. His undershirt was wet through, a testament to the state of his training. He was not weak willed or prissy, this prince of the thousand balls. She was desperately hoping he was weak willed, had some other tendency that she could look upon with scorn and derision. Every time she saw him, her heart fluttered and those damn feelings she shouldn't have felt but gave into on the forest road tried to consume her.

She smiled at the thought.

But he didn't smile.

Eli was finding that rather irksome.

His back was to her so he didn't notice her intense scrutiny, was unselfconscious in fiddling with the closures of his breeches and—

"You might want to keep those on for a moment."

So bashful, her prince.

He turned towards her intrusion, clasping the front placard of his trousers tightly closed. "How long have you been standing there?"

"Long enough to see you strip off your jerkin but no longer. I stopped you before you grew too interesting."

It was a definite difference between her people and his. Where she was used to the male form, having trained since birth to fight against them, sharing in the same summer ponds and bath houses with everyone else, his people were most strict on separation of the sexes. They built walls around walls around walls, city, home, and heart. Poor fools, and yet he didn't seem as perturbed by her appearance as she would have expected. Not that the light blush across his cheeks wasn't noticeable. He was very pretty when flushed.

"Was there something you needed or you just happened upon these quarters while investigating your new barracks?"

"The second, if you must know. I was looking for the baths." He didn't need to know she had her own in her chambers.

It was a likely excuse.

"They're underground. This is the royal wing."

"Which no one told me."

"And you asked who, precisely?"

She would have asked him, but the moment the general brought Kit's food, she was forgotten. "I know no one but you."

"Which precludes you from speaking to any others?"

"No."

He did not seem pleased by the admittance, or the disavowal, or whatever it was she was answering to. Damn, but she had no footing with him. Yes, with a sword in her hand, a knife in the other, she might be able to knock him back a peg, and he was quick enough to make it a match, at least until she grew bored and wanted the win. But this wasn't the man she'd spoken with the past three nights. The man who'd danced her around a ballroom filled with the most opulent of dresses in a rainbow of colors and her in black, darkest night, looking so out of place among the glittering throng.

"I'm sure they'd be accommodating if you voiced a question. As it is, I'm rather indisposed at the moment and would prefer my privacy to continue."

"I rather like this room and think I shall take a rest. Hard day's work and all that. Please, don't let me distract you."

She ensured her gaze held his while she moved into the room proper and took a seat on the bench where his change of clothes was laid out. Sitting put her eyes level with his naval, his height far greater than hers, though he was unsure of its advantage. Perhaps tomorrow she would show him that a smaller, lighter person could easily unbalance him and land him in a bind. It would prove a good lesson for the military corps in general. Well, she would not lie to herself and ignore that half the appeal of the lesson was watching her young prince beaten back.

"Really?" The incredulity in his tone brought her gaze to his.

She really must stop her mind from wandering. Not that wandering did much good, eventually she always came back to the present and the mess she'd made of her life. Funny, that said mess didn't feel so messy at all right now.

"This seat is quite comfortable. Go on, I promise, it's nothing I've not seen before."

She may have been mistaken, but she thought she caught a hint of anger in his gaze, along with the blush on his cheeks, at her mention of having seen other men undressed.

Rules of propriety: A woman and man mustn't meet before their mating.

Stupid city rules, all their walls they put up trying to keep themselves separate from the world and each other.

He'd barely worked up the nerve to kiss her and then that had been ruined by her brethren's interruption.

No. Not brethren. No more.

Her enjoyment in tormenting him dimmed with the thought.

There was something about him that called to her, begged to be tempted and pushed until all that he was overflowed and consumed her in the flood. The Darkness in her soul yearned for his light, and it was a strange yearning, almost peaceful in its craving.

"Fine then."

He met her gaze and did his best to hold it, mouth set in a grim line, eyes cold and stormy staring down at her. She let him think her caught, watching his fingers fumble at the ties of his breeches before he managed to push the cloth past his hips, small cloths remaining behind for a hint of modesty. Her eyes dropped to his waist, the trim hips, defined muscles his clothing covered so elegantly, even clothing meant for work fit him perfectly. If she'd said yes to him, if she'd given in to desire and left with him, all this flesh would be hers to touch and more.

When she stood, he stepped back, trying to keep space between them. It didn't occur to her not to follow, a predator stalking her prey. He continued to back away and she advanced until his knees struck against a second bench and it was her hand grabbing his arm that helped him steady. "You're more graceful on a dance floor."

"More room to spin in."

"Or flee."

"I don't flee."

"Liar."

He hadn't noticed that she'd taken his clothing in one hand, so focused on her approach he hadn't been watching her fingers. Another lesson for another day in the lists. Good, she was beginning to develop quite a curriculum to aid in protecting her new liege.

Eli wanted him to survive.

Who better than an assassin to train him so?

"Stand still, Prince. Best to get you changed before someone else barges in on us."

"There is no us."

"Precisely."

She sank slowly to her knees, ignoring the body before her in favor of focusing on the task at hand. With quick, efficient movements, she stripped him of his soiled garments, piling pants and undergarments together in one hand while she passed him his cleaned clothing with the other. A hamper lingered along one wall. She took advantage of the basket to deposit his practice clothes into while he pulled fresh breeches on. He sucked in his breath, stomach contracting into rippling muscle when she returned to him and laced him into his leathers.

She held his shirt out for him, and he snatched it from her hands too quickly.

"You don't smile like you did at the ball."

He stopped with his head stuck within the mess of cotton over his hair.

She couldn't help herself as she reached up and untangled his shirt, her hands running down his sides in the pretense of helping him dress. His arms remained in the air over his head while she touched him. For this moment, she did not meet his gaze, instead focusing on her fingers smoothing out the wrinkles in his tunic, tying the laces at his throat. He'd cover his shoulders with the blue jacket she'd left on the bench, hide this physique behind layers of cloth. She didn't understand this need to be covered, but, then again, walls were not only made of brick and mortar.

He swallowed, the bob of his Adam's apple drawing her gaze. Almost, she could imagine his head thrown back in passion, the way he would struggle for air, tortured by pleasure.

She shook her head, trying to clear it of the image.

"I smile."

His gaze found hers. She recognized the ploy for what it was. If her focus was on his face, then other things could be ignored. She let him distract her, though she could see the lowering of his arms from the corner of her eye, the way he leaned into the scant space between them even while the whispered words and the grim set of his lips hinted at the desire to escape.

"Not like you did at the ball."

"We are no longer at the ball, Captain. This is the real world again. There is no time for fancy twirls and grand costumes. You will have to grow used to the change same as anyone else."

That wasn't what she meant.

The change, as he so roughly put it, had nothing to do with the ball and gowns and aristocrats swelling the palace walls. The change had to do with him, the way his lips would tilt upwards at the corners, his teeth would sparkle in a beam of sunlight, and his eyes would remain dark and bruised to the flirting and the posturing and the politics around him. There was a hint of a smile in the fencing room this morning when he took his blade to the general and beat the man back rather soundly. Maybe even a hint when she disarmed him and then showed him how she'd managed the feat. But now his smile was the one he wore for the court, and it was not the smile he'd given her.

She missed that smile.

"Of course, Kit."

"Prince Christophe. Highness. Or My Lord, Captain. Never Kit. I will not tell you again."

The correction took her aback. They were in private. Surely he would not insist on such formality between them— but they were no longer at the ball, and she was no longer a woman whom he was asking to dance.

She killed her people to spare his life.

It was the killing of his heart that was the true wound.

"My apologies, my Prince."

He did not correct her claiming.

They stood facing each other, his garments in order, her slighter frame blocking him from his jacket and an exit from the room. If he wished her to move, then he would have to ask or push her from his way. She was used to silence and doubted he had suffered the same treatments in his life.

"Excuse me." His words were curt though proper in every way.

"Of course, my Prince."

She stepped easily aside.

He walked past her, picking up his coat and slinging it over his shoulders.

She held the door for him when he exited, followed in his wake the way a guard should.

"Are you planning on being my shadow the entire day?"

"Yes, Sir, it was my assigned task." Not precisely true. All right, it was almost entirely a lie. But he didn't need to know that. And besides, she was sure she could make a good excuse as to her presence. The prince's death had been prophesized for a long while, who was to say there was not an assassin waiting just around the corner to steal his life?

"You plan on entering the city in that?" He looked over his shoulder at her, eyes moving down her flowing shirt and the black breeches covering his legs.

If she wanted, she could be a shadow in the streets. Easier to be a shadow dressed in black than in skirts. "Yes."

He sputtered, unsure of how to respond.

"Is there something wrong with my attire? You didn't seem to have a problem with it during drills this morning?"

"That was drills—"

"Yes, and this is guard duty, not a grand ball or a picnic outing."

"Is that what you think I'm doing? Going on a picnic?"

"Dressed like that? I don't know what you're doing, my lord." She did not try to keep the sarcasm from her voice. Honestly, she rather liked the way he was dressed. He wore his fashions fitted enough that should he be in a fight, his clothing wouldn't hamper his movements. That they had the added benefit of endearing him to the feminine eye at the same time was not something she would share with him. He looked like he could go to a picnic or summit meeting or whatnot dressed the way he was.

He searched her face. It was disconcerting to be so studied, yet she stood her ground. This was not the study of the changing room, laced with a heat she didn't think he even recognized. This was something different, a soldier recognizing his opponent's skill. Why this perusal threatened to bring a blush to her cheeks and the other did not, she couldn't say, but she liked it.

"Fine. Tomorrow you're off guard duty."

"That is not your call to make, my lord." The pink in his cheeks was not from embarrassment this time. "I was assigned this duty by the general as I am the best at presenting an unassuming tail. I will be a ghost. I swear it. You will not even notice me there."

His teeth grit, jaw clenching, fighting back his instinctual denial of her demands. The play of emotion over his face was eloquent, and quick, too quick given that she would have enjoyed watching anger chase away embarrassment, fade to joy if she could manage to make him grin.

The blasted court smile turned his lips, eyes shadowed with anger. "Very well."

She liked his ire. It was refreshing from the solemn disinterest he'd shown her since their return to the palace. She liked it, but would not be swayed by it.

She'd keep her word and be his shadow.

He did not look behind him to see if she followed or not.

He would not have spotted her regardless.

Chapter II
One

K it couldn't forget her presence behind him.

She kept her word, and was like a shadow, blending so easily into the city around him that if he hadn't been tuned to her every movement, her every breath, he would have lost her entirely. He had to constantly remind himself not to stop and look for her, not to turn around and invite her into a conversation with him.

She wasn't the woman at the ball anymore.

How could he have been so stupid as to think three nights of dancing would have endeared him to her, or to any woman for that matter?

And she was an assassin.

Sweet gods, she could have killed him at any time if she so desired.

And when she trained with him that on his birthday—

He turned around, spun really, in the middle of the crowded street, left then right trying to find her.

She burst from her position against a wall, moving to his side with a speed he envied and a grace he could never hope to emulate. He grabbed her arms when she reached for a knife at her belt, a knife he didn't even know she had or how she'd come about its possession. "You were my opponent on Samseiet!"

Her lips parted but she spoke no words to him. He waited but she seemed unable to find her voice, not to affirm or deny his remark. She came to the fencing room before today. She'd come in trousers with her mock cock and her hair tucked beneath a cap that he'd found odd but hadn't questioned his young opponent. She'd come as a boy learning the art, not as one of his men well trained to the sword. And he'd stood opposite her, him, whatever, and parried gently so as to aid the boy's approach to the bout.

"Why?"

Her eyes rolled to his, chin tilting just far enough that he though she might be clenching her teeth, unsure if it was displeasure at his manhandling, or a vein of temper at being so questioned by him. Did she think he was unaware of her skill? Was that what her look was about? She held his stare and shrugged.

His lips drew back in an unhappy snarl and it took all his will not to shake her. "Why, Eli? To kill me before my men? Show how woefully unprepared we are for you and your kind?"

"My kind no more."

He didn't understand, didn't know why the tone of her voice caused a wave of pain to pierce his heart. "Why then?"

"To know you," her hands touched his elbows, completing the circle of their arms though he could not decide if it was intentional or some form of guardianship he was unfamiliar with. His soldiers rarely touched him except to pull him from whatever harm they suspected.

"And yet you were so against the knowledge yestereve."

The blush that came to her cheeks was nearly hidden, nearly undetectable if he wasn't so attuned to watching every subtle nuance of her face, so captivated by it. "It was two days ago, now."

"Damnit." He shook her, a gentle shake, his fingers lightening their hold on her arms so he didn't hurt her. "Do you truly think this has anything to do with when the conversation occurred? You lied to me, thrice over!"

"I never lied."

"You didn't tell the whole truth."

"You're a politician, Prince. You always tell the whole truth?"

He had no response to that, and damn her, he knew she saw that too.

"Push me away; throw me out, exile me from your kingdom, or allow me the job you offered and take your hands from my arms."

How sick of him to admire this anger of hers, this strength.

She was in the wrong. She had to know she was in the wrong and yet she acted like she had more right to her anger than he did his. She was the one who lied about who she was, invaded his palace, her woodsy ways so at odds with his culture. And she'd refused him when he offered her a chance at his hand.

That's what irked him most.

That she was the better swordsman was unquestioned. He had her in the ballroom. They both lied easily enough, convincingly enough to one another.

No, he had never lied.

Had he lied?

"Are you going to let go?"

Kit dropped his hands from her arms, stepping back quickly. The moment she came close, all reason deserted him. He was a prince, a politician, a soldier, a general. He knew better than to allow himself to be distracted, knew to listen first and speak second. Yet she interrupted him without regard, her words as pure as though there was no filter between her thoughts and her speech. Guileless, though secret filled.

And his heart still beat for her.

Of everything that had happened, that he could not remove her from his desires, that her betrayal, her lies and secrets and, for the gods sakes, her victories in the practice field, meant nothing to him when she was near, were the things he should not forgive, and yet could not hold against her.

He held her gaze, standing in the middle of the street as washer women and craftsmen and soldiers on patrol passed them by, said soldiers walking slowly to ensure he was not in need of assistance.

He shooed them and they quickened their pace.

"And if I exiled you, where would you go? Would you then pit your skills against mine? Return as my assassin in the dead of the night?"

"No." He didn't miss the way her voice grew hoarse at the suggestion, the flash of horror in her eyes that she might attempt to kill him. "I wouldn't return as your assassin."

A moment longer. He wanted a moment longer to look in her eyes, pretend that they weren't in some unknowable battle of wills, that he wasn't supposed to hate her and she wasn't supposed to hate him and that that flare in his chest meant nothing.

"Fine then."

He turned and walked away heading towards the center square and the vendors setting their wares out for the day. Already the fresh scent of baked bread and apple tarts layered the air. If nothing else, the smell calmed his raw nerves, recalled his childhood where he would sneak out of the palace and race to the marketplace and Cinta would pass Kit a sweet bun before going back to his oven.

He hadn't been to the baker in years.

Every time he thought to leave the palace for a moment, something else would come up: another meeting, a request by a steward for something or other, a noble wanting a quick word.

The only reason he managed a respite this afternoon was that he'd left before anyone could stop him. He never left straight from fencing, but she'd distracted him, turned his head, and now here he was in the city. Yes, he knew the palace was like a city unto itself, but he enjoyed walking the streets of Tornald, seeing the people, speaking to them. He wasn't going to live his life afraid to leave his rooms because there was a bounty on his head. His people protected him. He would honor that by proving he trusted them enough to be part of their lives and not remain secluded from them.

Pigeons swooped around the baker's stall, the breads and rolls lining the table did not rise to their usual appeal. The red of the awning hung partway open, like it had been done in a hurry and not done well. The baker himself was nowhere in sight.

Cinta had never been so lazy or so lax in his shop's appeal.

Kit stepped towards the stall and frowned when her hand closed around his upper arm, drawing him to a stop. He looked back at her, and she nodded to the ground and the dead pigeon and two dead rats half hidden beneath the wrinkled tablecloth covering the stand.

His hand went to the sword at his hip, and again she stopped him, stepping up to his side rather than the foot behind she'd been following.

She turned so that she faced him, keeping her lips averted from the store's front window. "I need you to slap me and walk away in a huff, find the patrol that passed us and get back to the palace."

"That's not happening, Captain."

"Something's not right here, you know it as well as I."

"Yes, and Cinta and his family have been friends of mine for years. I'm not leaving until I know what's wrong. They wouldn't betray me."

"They might not have had a choice."

"All the more reason to stay." But he understood the need to playact a scene, not to rouse more suspicion around them than his being prince already did. He pushed her hand from his arm, turned to walk towards the stall as was his original intent. He wouldn't actually get close to the thing, just close enough that it appeared he was oblivious to the threat.

"Sweet Darkness."

He heard the whispered curse behind him before her arm came from his back to wrap around his throat, her knife pressed against his pulse. A quick jab to his side had him bending at his middle to protect the injury, not having expected the attack, not prepared for it. He doubled over, seeing spots, wondering if this was all an act or if he'd put his faith in the wrong person.

"The bounty's mine, you bastards."

He struggled at that, fighting to pull away, lash out. She was quick enough to avoid his attempt, pin an arm at the small of his back, press up on his captured wrist until he rose on his toes, trying to relieve the strain on his shoulder while she forced the appendage at its unnatural angle. Kit fought to control his breathing, unable to look up as she held him bent over, the knife at his throat precluding him from turning his head to try and read the situation.

"You should have killed me in the forest."

"Shut up, your highness."

She held him prisoner to her, slowly relaxing her grip until the hand captured at his back slipped to her waist, the knife holstered there, her fingers helping his to curl around the hilt, hidden between their bodies. The weapon did nothing to relax him, only tensing his muscles further, undecided if she was friend or foe, praying for friend.

She bent towards him, a quick look beneath his bowed spine, to his sides, her face hidden by his body. "Play along, Kit, or we're both dead."

The withheld breath eased from his chest, letting the simple command calm him, knowing he shouldn't trust this woman and unable to stop himself at the same time.

He didn't know what had spooked her, didn't know how to ask.

But the door to the baker's crashed open. Three huffed breaths, three rancid scents, filled the small street, stormed from the room and shifted over the cobblestones, drawing neither closer nor backing away. She pressed up on his bound arm, forcing his bend more severely, minimizing the target he presented, no clear sight line to his heart from behind, her body a shield from the side and front. She'd relaxed her knife enough for him to see the situation but maintain her capture, his gaze just able to pick out the unshaved faces looking at him, the hint of more boots out of his peripheral vision.

He heard the table clatter to the ground, a poisoned roll rolling towards his feet, splintered wood having crossed the cobblestones to land near his boots, evidence of the violence of the men's approach.

Three men.

She'd taken four without problem.

He could hold his own in a fight, despite what she might think.

But this wasn't about killing the enemy.

Kit knew the faces of his townsfolk, knew the men and women who worked outside the palace walls and within the city limits, those who'd come before the king begging sanctuary, who'd pledged their allegiance to Kit when they were given shelter.

These men did not belong here.

That there was no alarm suggested that their arrival had gone unnoticed. And if their arrival was unnoticed, perhaps the baker and his wife and son were alive within the small house.

How long would these bastards have spent hoping to catch Kit out about the city? He never kept to a schedule. There was no one who knew he'd left that afternoon but his guards, and they were discreet. None had left before him except the group they'd passed, and they were gone before he even escaped the palace that day.

Her body stiffened next to his, tension or hesitation, he couldn't decide until the pressure of the knife changed and she forced him to straighten, allowed him a view of the street around them, the men circling their position.

"Tell the rest of your men to come out. You five aren't worth my time."

Shit.

The tailor from across the street, the bookseller's and the printing press, disgorged their cohort of mercenaries, enough that even with the guards walking the city, Kit and Eli would likely die.

Twenty men against two. If his guards came, that added five to their side. That she had a knife to his throat was buying them time, but not nearly enough.

"Looks to me like we've got the better claim to the lad, elf."

"Looks to me like you have more men and think that makes your claim better." He heard the cruelty in her words, the edge he didn't know how to respond to. "In truth, it makes the split of the bounty smaller, which is why I always work alone."

She took a step back and Kit followed with her, allowing her to move him where she would, his strings pulled taut. The men at their backs shifted, stepping forward to threaten her retreat. Her lips pressed to his throat, teeth pressing into her skin in threat; her knife drew a small line beneath his jaw. She tsked at the mercenaries, smiling against Kit's skin. "Do you know who I am, hunter?"

The man paused, looked her over, shrugged. "Another elf looking to make a name for himself." He waved a hand in the air, dismissing her. "Passed your kind on our way in. They were smart enough to wish us luck on the kill, Precious. You should run back to them."

Kit felt her stiffen against him, her people responsible for their present circumstances, or at least instigating it to move along faster. They didn't attack themselves, but free reign to others apparently.

She made no verbal response. He couldn't decide if her playing assassin or keeping her name hidden would spare them. Not that it mattered when she drew a second line of fire over his skin, thin, not much blood, barely a scratch but enough of a threat for the men around them and his focus returned to the moment rather than debating the merits of irrelevant thoughts.

"You kill him, we kill you, the bounty is ours and there's plenty of time on the road between here and Kirbi for men to die."

That the merc made the threat before said men acknowledged how fragile the confederacy between them.

Kit wondered if their destination of Kirbi was a lie.

The island continent was across the sea. No one came from there but hired swords. Their bounty would not come from the other country; their master hidden somewhere closer to Kit's home.

He hissed when she pressed his arm further up his back. "I'm willing to split the bounty five ways, boys. Maybe throw in something special for the lads that help a poor lass out." His body reacted without thought to the implication, struggling in her grip which she ensured the gathered men noticed her hold on him, how easy killing him would be. "Best make that decision fast gentlemen, before I lose patience." He couldn't decide what angered him more, that she would offer sex as a reward to his potential killers, or that she refused him in the same.

He didn't want that with her though. He wanted more. He—

She'd kept them moving, her steps even, steady, unhurried and ignored by their hunters. The tanner's shop was at their backs. A heavy kick to the door, a fast retreat, and mayhap they'd find some safety in the small house until reinforcements found them.

If she was with him, and this wasn't a ploy.

Stop thinking!

The leader drew a crossbow from his accomplice, aimed the weapon at Kit's chest. "Twenty against one, little miss. It's been a lark carryin' on like we 'ave, but we've wasted enough time now."

With a smile, the mercenary fired at the same moment Eli pushed Kit aside. The crossbow bolt thudded into the heavy wood behind them.

Kit didn't stumble away, using her push to spin around, her dagger in his hand, let fly against the leader while she kicked the door in. He followed her into the room, overturning the cabinet inside the threshold to act the barricade to the broken latch. The wood would hold for a time, enough deterrent that the best avenue of advance into the space was through the windows, bottlenecking the men attacking, their advantage of numbers minimized.

Her knives flashed in the dim sunset of the room, slicing through the shattering of glass to strike the first man through. Kit pulled the sword from his hip, barely enough room for him to raise the weapon against the male sent tumbling towards him when she passed the mercenary back for Kit to finish. A quick slice, empty hands raised to the red smile cut along the male's throat, and Kit turned his head to his next opponent.

The table at Kit's back threatened to trip him, acted to the killer's benefit when Kit was forced against the wooden surface, rendering his sword useless. His fingers scrabbled against the table, searching for anything to use against the man atop him. A handle slipped into Kit's fist, and he didn't care what it was, swinging wildly against the man, ignoring the momentary shock of blood spraying over him when the knife slashed the carotid and the man died above him.

Kit's fingers tightened against the weapon, both hands full of metal to meet the next attack, unable to spare a moment to see how Eli fared at the front.

Horns sounded in the street.

The ground shook beneath the clomp of hooves. Soldiers sent to join the fray.

The mercenaries stuck within the tanner's with him and Eli tried to flee, but there was no other exit from the small room. Kit swung high, took the head of one man, watched her sink two knives into her opponent's sides, draw the weapons up, slice the belly open. The man dropped.

Kit leaned against the table, trying to catch his breath amidst the dying men at his feet. His gaze scanned the decimated bodies, counting the dead they'd slain.

His eyes closed at Marius' shout. "We're clear out here, my prince."

But "clear" was not enough. "How many mercenaries out there?" Her words echoed around the room, spinning through his brain.

He tried to lift his head, stare at anything but the blood soaked ground at their feet, but it was difficult, so difficult, each breath a challenge in itself. Her hands cupped his cheeks, raised his gaze to hers. He hadn't seen her move towards him. "Are you hurt?" The soft whisper of her words broke the spell in his head, the catch of her eyes with his.

"Nothing serious."

One hand slid from his cheek to the red staining his left arm, drifted to the blooming gash on his side beneath the linen shirt he wore.

"We've seven here, Captain."

"There are nine in here with us."

She nodded at Kit's words but didn't relay the message outside, her gaze held on his slight wound, fingers pinching at the skin, making him hiss.

He turned his head to the chamber, searching corners, counting bodies again, anything but looking at her. "I counted twenty men out there."

"Twenty-one, there was a rat on the roof above us, too young to be part of their brotherhood, but a member all the same."

"A lookout?"

"A spy."

"That's five men unaccounted for." He said.

Her cheeks twitched in what might have been a grin but never fulfilled the promise of false gaiety it strove for. "What are the odds we've made them rethink the bounty on your head?"

He gave her a grim smile in return. "You did a good job of ensuring they wouldn't, Captain." Her brow furrowed at his response. "Less to split the bounty between now."

"Shit."

Marius entered the small room, hands held wide, intending no harm. Kit's arm rose, sword ready for another attack despite the approach of his friend. The arm she'd been examining tightened around her, pulling her close lest the known general prove less than trustworthy.

The commander dropped to his knees before Kit, ignoring the woman standing as shield in front of the prince's body. "I've failed you, your highness."

Kit met the dismal gaze leveled on him, his grip relaxing across Eli's shoulders. "I'm alive."

"I should have sent guards with you."

"You didn't know I was leaving." Kit stared down at his general, tsked when the man failed to look up. "You got here in time to save our lives. Find the rest of the bastards and consider the debt paid."

Marius rose, eyes scanning the room now that he was forgiven by his prince. "More?"

She spoke. "At least five within the city. Not counting if they had others waiting beyond the walls."

Marius turned his gaze to Eli, the elf unflinching beneath the glare. "I heard you had a knife to Kit's throat."

"I heard I saved his life from those who would have taken it without my knife there."

No trust between them then, and perhaps Kit shouldn't be as trusting of her as he was.

"She's my captain, General, named and witnessed by you and our men. She saved my life."

Blue eyes landed on the red stain at Kit's throat, though how Marius could see the small gash beneath the flow of blood from their adversaries was beyond Kit. Too much blood.

The slice at his side burned; the one along his sword arm was numb so long as he didn't move but flared hot with agony any time he adjusted his grip on his weapon. Eli'd already surveyed the nick to his left bicep.

Would mercenaries resort to poison? Or would that be too hard to prove who made the kill?

A lifetime spent with the threat of death over his head, and this was the first time he'd ever taken a life in defense of his own.

"Kit."

Marius stepped forward, and Kit took a moment to close his eyes, gain control of his breathing, ignore the stench of the dead and dying, of blood and spilled guts around him. It bothered him, to have had to take a life, but worse would have been dying and fulfilling the demise of his city through prophecy.

She stepped to his side, her fingers wrapping around his forearm, the trembling in his limb from over exertion. She clenched her hand, and he flinched at the bite of her nails in his skin. Marius ripped a hank of the hem of his shirt off, bound the cloth around Kit's right arm, a makeshift bandage until they reached the palace.

The two worked smoothly together when he was the focus of their energy.

"Are you all right? Do you think the blades were poisoned?"

He shook the arms off him, pushed against the table so that he could stand on his own, force his soldiers away to give him room.

Marius edged Eli aside.

The snarl she leveled at the commander had Kit's head snapping to the woman.

"Enough. Whatever it is between you, put it aside." He made sure to meet both of their eyes, hold them in his glare. "I trust her same as I trust you—"

"She held a knife to your throat!"

"Yes, and she had me alone against four of her brethren and saved my life at the cost of theirs." He didn't intend to raise his voice, so very rarely lost his temper that it was a shock to his system as much as his soldiers.

Kit closed his eyes, breathed in, waited for the world to calm a moment before he continued. Marius wasn't the only one at fault; at least, Kit didn't think Marius was the only one at fault. He'd address the issue regardless. "She's ours now, sworn to me. You don't have to like her, but you will accept her as it is my order for you to do so, Marius. She's proven herself more than an ally. She didn't have to fight to save my life the first time, but she did." He turned his gaze to Eli. "And you: Marius earned the title of General of my guard and my army. He has dedicated his life to its service, to me, and deserves the respect owed him for earning his position. He might fight differently than you, he might have lived differently than you, but you are both warriors and will respect each other as such. Am I clear?"

"I know how to protect against assassins better than he does."

"Only because you were one—"

"Yes, because I *was* one." She met Marius furious gaze, met the incredulous tone with the vehement truth of her own.

Kit watched the mask come down over her emotions, veiling her anger or whatever else she felt behind it. Whether she was trying to obey his decree to play fair with the general, or if it was her natural way to hide how she felt, she was giving Marius a direct stare, unchallenging even as it was dominant.

"If I hadn't put my knife to his throat, they would have had a clean shot at his back. Keeping my body between them and his saved his life. If I hadn't put a knife to his throat, they wouldn't have hesitated to kill us both; but another mercenary against them left room for doubt because, despite it all, General, mercenaries and assassins follow a code of honor. It might not be the honor you appreciate, but it is there. I had first claim to him then. They had the numbers over me. Putting my knife to his throat was the only way to buy us time to get into a position where we wouldn't be at such a disadvantage, where we had a chance of lasting until you got here."

Kit watched his commander clench his jaw, a tick working at the man's right eye.

"What would you suggest we do now, Assassin?"

"Captain, Marius. She gave you your title," Kit snapped

"Assassin is appropriate, my prince."

Kit closed his eyes, his head throbbing from more than just the fighting.

"Their leader should be wounded, upper body, maybe head. I don't think it was fatal but left untreated it might be. Whoever is left will flock to him, so we find him, we find them. The problem will be whether they decide to risk attacking right off, or wait a night or two hoping our guard lowers." She looked away from Marius' stare, pulling her bloodied knives from their sheaths at her hips to clean the blades of some of their blood along the linen of her trousers. The action drew Marius' attention to the red she'd spilled in Kit's defense, another reminder that she'd been the key to Kit's life. The motion was neither subtle, nor unintentional.

Kit watched Marius swallow back his pride.

"If it were you, Captain?"

She replaced the weapons in the sheaths at her sides. "If it were me, I wouldn't have brought twenty men to do a job a slim knife in a passerby's hand could accomplish. Barring that, I'd strike again, fast. I'd move with the light, hiding in plain sight, unexpected, but they're scared, they'll wait till full dark."

"So in Kit's chambers."

"Likely so."

"We'll put guards on the doors and below the balcony."

"On the balcony. They had a man on the roof. It's possible they'll try that way again." Both soldiers turned to look at Kit, apparently realizing he was privy to their conversation. That it was Marius' stare that held disbelief at Kit's words, and Eli's that held approval, did not endear the man to Kit.

"I know you don't like anyone in your rooms, Kit—"

That it was for Kit's comfort Marius hesitated with the guards eased some of the ice in Kit's gut. "There will be a threat until I'm five hundred and eighteen years old, Marius. I'm not going to be coddled my whole life. Until these men are captured, you'll have the rule of me, but once it's done, we go back to how we were."

"That wasn't particularly safe, my—"

"Though I named you captain, Captain, in this I do not require your opinion to guide me. I will not be a prisoner in my own country. I won't cower."

"Then you'll learn to fight."

He frowned at the woman who looked so calm and serene covered in blood fiddling with the hilt of a dagger stuck in her belt. "I know how to fight."

"Like your people, yes." She focused her gaze on his face and it was Kit who turned aside. "You'll learn to fight like mine. Like the Dienobolos. Like the Quifolno and their desert-men brothers from Kirbi. I'll teach you the way of the island people of Wen, the Kirannas and the Tuabs, the warriors of Zahni."

Kit snorted at her list, the fantasy of it. "Why not add the lost people of Miest to the list then? Or, perhaps you've seen fairies fluttering about your woods you'd like me to train with?" He could not help the sarcasm in his voice.

Yes, his father had opened trade routes with the Islands of Wen and the desert land of Kirbi. Hells, those same trade routes likely brought his current attackers to Spinick's shores.

Prutwl even sent delegations upon a time, but the crossing to the northern continent was more hazardous and Leon hadn't approved those shipping lanes yet.

But the "warriors of Zahni," the desert dancers of Quiofol, no one knew their fighting styles. They were closed territories, they'd never waged war against Spinick or his father or his father's father. No one knew their ways of battle, not even the once Elichisolos of the Dienobolos.

Or was that just a hope in his heart? If she knew all that she suggested, then how in the gods names would he stop her?

"The people of Miest left the dragon lands long ago. What's left of their culture is not something to mock, Prince. They're deadly. They had to be. They killed enough great serpents on Zephra to make the land slick with black blood and they survived to tell the tale of it."

She spoke like she knew such men and women.

Zephra was a dead land.

Its people were dead.

But the Dienobolos worshipped the Darkness, so mayhap they walked the shores of the afterlife like it was simply the twilight of this world.

Her anger had the ring of righteousness to it.

"My apologies, my lady. I meant no offense."

She nodded, releasing him from the razor of her glare. "I wouldn't teach you the ways of the Miestians, Prince. You're too faint of heart."

That raised his hackles, and he wanted to retort, but the look in her gaze suggested that, though she might have learned the mythical art of war of the dragon people, even she was not comfortable in its use. He bowed his head, acquiescing to her knowledge on the subject.

He looked to Marius, the shrewd look in the man's eyes, the distrust and raging hunger for the things she suggested and Kit had little faith in. Kit would suffer for that hunger, forced to train unnaturally to fulfill the general's desire for military acumen. Kit would suffer the training fields and the healer's touch because she was staring at him too, and her eyes held a similar hunger, one far more personal or so it seemed.

"We should get back to the palace."

"Yes."

Eli agreed, led them from the confines of the death filled room.

Kit mounted the horse presented to him, rode through the streets at a gallop, no one willing to let him linger longer in the unprotected and unknown alleys of his home city.

At least no one would be training in new doctrines today.

For once, he almost looked forward to the solitude of being locked in his own chambers.

Two

He slipped the knife under his pillow, stretched his arms over his head, and flinched when the right protested the movement. His side ached beneath the bandage wrapped tight round his middle, his muscles opposing the strain, wanting simply to relax from the tension of the day. His mind wouldn't relax. Kit doubted his body would.

He'd foregone any bedclothes for the evening, preferring to sleep beneath the sheets comfortably despite the chill outside his windows. He'd kept his breeches on; a lingering worry that Eli might be correct, that his would-be assassins would strike again during the night and he didn't want to be without some decency covering his skin.

Guards stood outside his balcony. He'd offered them blankets for warmth since they were not allowed fire. They'd politely refused, something about the cold being bracing, and shut his balcony doors, closing him inside his chambers. Guards were at the doors to his sitting rooms, at the doors that connected his room to the second set of family quarters, at the main doors of his suite and his bedroom, all doors closed and all guards sworn to keep careful watch throughout the night. No doors locked in case they had to invade quickly. Easy access for any who made it past the men though

If any of the men died, it would be in his defense.

Marius would say they died doing their duty or they died because they hadn't trained hard enough.

Kit suspected that Eli would hold a similar mindset.

He settled on his back beneath the blankets. The pillows mounded enough behind his head that he had a clear view of his room. The bed curtains wound tight to their banisters, leaving ample space to escape the large four posters and anyone coming to attack.

A guard had even checked beneath the bed and beneath the sheets in case someone had slipped something into his room without his notice.

He'd been confined to the damn space for the entirety of the evening upon returning to the palace. The only one who could have slipped something into the room was Kit, and he hadn't done that. He had no desire to die.

His eyes drifted closed; he turned on the mattress so that he was practically buried between the soft blankets, head cradled within the mound of pillows.

His hand curled on the hilt of the dagger.

❧

He kept his breathing deep and steady, no hint that he was awake or aware of his surroundings.

The first thump had been nearly silent, but to heightened nerves had sounded obscenely loud in the confines of his room.

There hadn't been a struggle, and now there was silence once more from the balcony.

His eyelids cracked open enough to allow him a glance towards the glass doors, the shades drawn to keep out the torchlight and the sight of the men beyond the windows. He should have kept the damn things open.

His sword was against the nightstand, close enough that a quick flip would find the blade in his hand, but enough time for a quarrel to find its way to his heart from a crossbow.

The handle of the door turned, visible only in the flickering light of the few candles Kit had left burning on his desk.

There was no bow in the hands that entered the room first, only black gloves followed by an equally black uniform, even the face shadowed by cloth. The mercenary clung to the shadows, moving along the wall towards Kit's bed without stepping out into the open of the room. It kept the man in Kit's sight, poor fool.

Kit's fingers clenched around his knife and the man pressed a knee to the bed. Kit's wrist jerked up and out, slipping through the cloth at the man's throat, into the flesh beneath. Warm liquid splashed over Kit's face and he closed his eyes, trying not to think about the assassin dying in his bed, the men slain earlier that day by his hand.

The mercenary's blade thudded against the quilt, fingers gone nerveless in his last minutes of life.

Kit squirmed from beneath the male's weight, slipped over the side of the bed without rising, presenting as small a target as possible.

His eyes went back to the balcony door, left open now with no one to close it.

Had someone else come into his room in the moment before his attacker died? Was he even now being stalked unaware while the first assassin cooled?

A shadow slipped from the porch, thin and willowy, moving quickly to the bed, not trying to hide its approach.

There would be no surprise this time. The attacker would know Kit was alive the moment he pulled his sword from the sheath.

He stood with the blade drawn, drew the mercenary's gaze though Kit did not attack directly.

Shadows cleared, and Eli crouched at the side of the bed. A quick glance to him, noting he lived, was unharmed, and her eyes turned to the corpse. "You survived."

"I'm not incompetent."

"No, you're not." She pulled the assassin's hood off his head, adjusted the corpse so that he looked like he was simply sleeping rather than sprawled where he lay.

Kit watched her pull the sheets over the body before stepping away.

"The guards on the balcony are dead. I managed to kill the one climbing the wall but another came from over the roof before I could make the ascent."

"I'm assuming that's the one I killed then."

"Likely."

He didn't like the uncertainly in her response, but didn't question it either.

His gaze moved to the other doors to the room. "How many of them could be left? Three?"

"There were more in the outlying parts of the city in case you went to somewhere other than the baker's. There are at least thirty men looking to kill you."

"Why are they so determined? So long as I die before my five hundredth birthday, the city falls. They have time."

"Maybe their lord decided he couldn't wait another four hundred years. Or perhaps he rewards failure harsher than we would reward the attempt."

"In other words—?"

"We might kill them fast, where the master will kill them slowly."

A harsh reality, and one he couldn't refute. She spoke the truth, though if he survived, if any of the men survived the attempt of taking his life, Kit doubted his father would sanction a quick death for any of them.

He slipped away from the bed and into the deeper shadows near the hallway door, back against the wall to watch the room, conceal his presence. She had made a decoy of him in the bed. He'd best use the distraction.

His voice was barely a whisper, but the silence in the room offered no challenge to the hearing of the words. "You're sure it's a male?"

"The lord?" She smiled in the dim light of the room, moving from the bed to follow him into the corner, standing with her shoulder pressed to his against the wall. "A woman wouldn't fail. We're more vicious than men, crueler. You'd die, and yes, we'd obey and it would be timely, but it would be painful, that quick death, if called for by a woman." A chill slid down his spine at the ambivalence in her voice. "It's a male."

His throat was dry when he responded, doing his best for levity, to ignore the knowledge with which she spoke, the death stalking him. "Sexist."

"Realist."

"I yield to the greater experience."

Another flash of a smile and she turned towards the doors to the second set of apartments, staring hard at the wood separating them.

"How many guards were supposed to be out there?"

His breathing stilled at the question, his chest aching at the implication. "Two at each door."

"There is only one that way."

He almost asked how she could tell, but managed to refrain, unsure he wanted to know if she was using magic.

Oh, he knew about magic. The mages in the city cast spells over the palace once a year that protected it from weather damage. Supposedly the city itself was protected from direct attack, the enchantment built into the walls themselves. Kit knew some mages worked on close magic, magic that worked physically on the people it impacted, and then there were those who worked on inanimate objects, and those who could heal, and there were no dark mages in Spinick, but that didn't account for the other nations of Lornai.

She worshipped the Darkness Itself.

She was an assassin.

What magic would a dark mage wield if they were to call upon it?

"There is one shadow moving beyond that door, and three in the halls outside your room. That accounts for only six men including the two already dead."

"Where are the others?"

Her eyes met his.

"Can you find them, Captain?"

Her head tilted to the side, staring beyond him.

He watched the green of her iris bleed into the white of her eyes, fade beneath the black of her pupil until the whole of her eye was the same vitreous shade of shadow. If she scanned the room, he couldn't tell. If it was her eyes that were actually seeing, he didn't know. Her head turned, sharp, fast movements, a bird hunting its prey, left, right, up, down. Had she turned her head all the way around, Kit didn't know that he'd be able to abide that. The blackness of her gaze was disconcerting enough.

Slowly, minutely, her pupils began to recede, or perhaps it truly was shadows that were clearing from her vision as the whites and then the green reformed in her eyes.

"They're fighting in the main galley. A distraction for the six sent for you."

"And the guards around my room?"

"I do not think any are left this side of the living."

He cursed. He prayed. "Atha take them."

She said nothing to his fervent whisper, though her gaze turned away as though she couldn't abide his worship where he said nothing of hers. "I do not know your Atha."

"She was the Goddess of War."

"Was?"

He did not respond to her question, not knowing how to, even if he could. Atha was the goddess of war. But his faith was shaken with his mother's death. He resented her patron goddess, even as he offered the prayer to the Woman.

He raised his hand, brushing against the ash on her cheeks, smeared across her forehead, looking for a safer distraction than the gods he worshipped, the Darkness she prayed to. "Did you roll in a fireplace?"

"The cinders help to hide my face in the darkness."

"And you know this how?"

"Do you really want that answer?"

No, he didn't think he did. "Gods," he cursed, not knowing who else to call upon, how else to relieve his pent up fear and anger.

"Only one, and the Darkness is begging to claim a prize." She touched the blade of her knife to her lips, kissing the bloodied metal before flipping the hilt in her hand so the tip rested along her forearm, a deadly vambrace. "Do not engage unless they get past me."

There was no time to respond, or perhaps her timing was simply that impeccable. The door rattled and bowed inward, three men from the hall rushing through the mess in tandem with the single mercenary from the servant's entrance.

Kit's hand gripped harder around the hilt of his sword, the blade pointed towards the ground, unable to raise it with her so close. He watched the swing and parry and lunge of her knives, the mercenaries' grunts when she struck them, two downed without chance of rising, the last two advancing together against her.

The moment the one engaged, the other dropped away, slipping beneath her guard, trusting his fellow to distract the lady while he went for Kit.

But Kit had killed men that day.

His men had died for him this night.

The man lunged, and Kit stepped to the side, the blade passing safely beneath his arm, never slicing him as he turned, the swordsman's grasp weak enough that the hilt slipped from the man's grip, and Kit's blade buried in the mercenary's gut.

The would-be assassin clenched at the sword in his stomach, unaware of the further injury inflicted as Kit withdrew his weapon and turned to meet his captain's stare over the body.

"I showed you that move once and already you're putting it to use. That's unwise to the extreme, Prince. You need to practice. Instinct is one thing, but skill another."

"Maybe I have both."

"You do, but those skills are untested, and instinct isn't honed. I'll add that to the list of what we'll be working on come morning."

"And will I be wearing cinders while we go about blooding each other, Ella?"

She caught her breath and it took him a moment to realize the name he'd called her.

She responded before he could apologize. "No."

The pounding of his heart eased, the noise of it calming so that the sounds of battle from outside reached them, the fighting having progressed inside the walls of the palace if he had to guess.

Their position was compromised, the doors unable to hold back the wind let alone a soldier intent on the kill. She didn't even bother trying to salvage the wreck, leading him from his rooms, creeping silently down the halls. He didn't dare try to meet her gaze again, afraid it would be dark black pools that stared back at him.

They came to a crossway, silent like the dead behind them, yet she didn't lead him further. Her knives rose, one coming to cross his chest, press him to the stone behind her, far from the little light the dying torches cast into the small space. He sank to a crouch without her command, eyes trained above him where a soldier's gut might be, a raised sword prepared to attack.

She came up under the man's guard, barely stopping the advance of her knife into vulnerable throat as Marius aimed his crossbow at her. She pushed the bow aside and the general's eyes scanned the hall.

"Kit?"

"Here. Is there anywhere safe?"

"The last of the fighting is in the courtyard. All those who marched into the palace are dead. We ensured that."

"Did you keep one alive?" His general looked down at him, and Kit rose slowly, careful to keep his shadow from elongating with the torch.

The commander and captain's head were on a constant swivel, looking over each other's shoulders for attackers at their backs. They might not be fond of each other, but over a common foe, they worked in tandem. Kit filed the thought away for later reflection.

"Whoever survives the square will meet with questioning."

"Did you tell your men to leave one alive?"

"It didn't need to be said, Kit. We know whose life is at stake. We won't fail you."

Kit scowled. "It's not about failing me. Mine is not the only life at risk. How many of my men have died tonight? Men whose only crime was being sent to guard me while I slept? How many souls are on my head for them?"

"They didn't die protecting you."

His eyes narrowed on the woman before him. Marius' glare equally cold at her words.

"They died protecting this kingdom. Your fate is not your own, Prince. To disdain their sacrifice, to think it so miniscule, is disrespectful. They died to save this country. You lived to do the same. Honor that spirit, instead of acting the whiny brat."

The reprimand was on his tongue. A servant, a soldier, daren't speak to his, or her, prince that way. But he could not deny that she was right, and if nothing else, Marius' silence confirmed her avowal. "My apologies, Captain."

She hadn't looked at him, not even to rebuff him.

She didn't meet his gaze now, striding past Marius and into the hall beyond.

Soldiers formed along the walls, bloodied and tired, but alive and triumphant. Some were kept standing by the brace of a brother at their sides; others slumped against the stone, knees trembling, eyes haunted. There had been no wars to fight since Kit was born. Small attacks on the country, on the capital, but nothing that required the troops train in the field, learn the lesson and the pain of taking a life.

Kit met the gazes of many of the men, wondering if he bore the same haunted look in his eyes reflected back at him.

Three

The king stood on the steps of the palace, crown in place though he wore a simple night robe rather than his coat and sashes of the court. He nodded to Kit, eyes widening at the blood on Kit's chest, the bareness of the flesh revealed. Kit almost shrugged, but decided the gesture would be irreverent considering the scent of blood in the air and the cries of pain from the men lingering on this side of the veil in the courtyard below.

"We have sought no quarrel with you. We are a peaceful people and yet you brought this terror to our doors in the middle of the night. Our brothers are dead, their lives stolen by the recklessness of a few." King Leon looked to Kit, accepted Kit's bow of deference. "Tonight, we show no mercy. Let those who would make us enemies know we will not yield to their evil or their greed."

The guards took up a chant, hailing their king's wisdom, his anger on their behalf.

Kit focused on the men wrapped in irons, in ropes, some unable to rise, some whose eyes blazed with icy fury, wanting to kill, uncaring of the fate they faced.

"Death to the Prince!"

The lone voice was familiar, drew Kit's gaze to the wall surrounding the outer courtyard of the keep, the man standing alone atop the stone, crossbow in hand, the sun rising behind his back until he was just a shadow come to kill.

The whistle of the bolt reached him over the stricken crowd.

He couldn't see the quarrel though the sound of its passage seemed inordinately loud in the wide space.

Kit raised his hand, whether to bat the bolt away or block the sun so that he could see Death's coming, he didn't know.

He needn't have bothered.

Guards swarmed the tower where the leader stood, a bandage over the left side of his face, likely Kit's doing from the afternoon. The man didn't wait to be overtaken, flinging himself from the wall and laughing the short drop to his death. He struck the ground, and was silent though soldiers surrounded him just the same.

Kit looked at the hand hovering before his chest, the quarrel that pierced the center of her fist, caught without a nick to her own flesh, held at bay from piercing his.

Leon stared at Kit, eyes roving between him and the woman who was his guard. "Seize the witch!"

"Not on your lives!"

Kit put himself between Eli and his father. Marius moved to guard the lady's back.

"She is the captain of my guard, Father."

Irrational hate filled the king's gaze. "She's an elf!"

"She saved my life thrice over. Would you reward her with a noose?"

Leon took the step up, Kit's height allowing him to stare over his father's head, though the man had a large enough presence that Kit barely managed the feat. "She will kill you."

"She has killed for me."

The older man's stare ranged from Kit's face to Eli's to Marius, silently asking the commander to what, Kit couldn't guess. "You trust this woman?"

Marius looked down at Eli, and Kit glanced over his shoulder, begging the man to side with him for he spoke the truth. "She's saved him when I would have been too late to do the deed myself. Do I trust her?" Marius shrugged. "No, but she's done nothing to earn my distrust either."

"An elf can never be trusted. Her people were the most violent against you as a babe, Christophe."

Kit and Marius looked to the king's brother slowly descending the steps. Kravn's face held no expression, though there seemed a madness in his eye as he looked between elf and prince and back again.

"You are unharmed, Uncle?"

"No mercenary would dare attack the Wolf of Spinick."

Yes, the Wolf of Spinick, but Kit had never heard of mercenaries fearing anything before, especially not a man so far from his prime as the king's brother.

If Kravn was not attacked, likely it was because the older man had hidden far from the battle, though Kit would not say such to disrespect his kin.

"Of course, Uncle." Kit nodded appropriately, no sarcasm or pity in his voice.

Marius drew Leon's gaze from the family reunion, back to the woman whose fate they were deciding. "I vouch for her, my King."

"As I vouch for her, Father."

Leon's gaze moved to her. Eli held her arm upraised, the quarrel in her grasp unnoticed while her eyes roamed over the crowd, guarding Kit even as she was discussed.

"The Children of the Wood will not part with one of their own lightly."

"I am foresworn, King Leon."

She'd made the choice herself, to part with her brethren. Kit held his breath at her remark.

The monarch's eyebrows rose at so direct an address.

Kit said nothing to this new battle of wills.

"That does not endear you to me, girl."

Kit could not see her face, though he thought he heard the smile in her voice. "I am foresworn, King Leon, for saving your son from my kinsmen. Your general was witness to the aftermath."

"I saw her sword pierce one of the villains' hearts while the prince was vulnerable, my King."

"I trust her, Father."

Finally the King's gaze broke from the woman in question. "On your heads be it. But I will not have a girl guarding my son; put her on rounds, city watch, away from him even if he wishes her in his service."

"I am the most qualified of your men. You may ask your general if you do not trust my words."

"And you should learn to hold your tongue in my presence."

Kit had the feeling that his father held little glory over those she'd grown up with.

She was, had been, head of the judiciary of her people. Elichi. Elichisolos. He knew the name, the title he'd kept from Marius. He knew before she told him on the ride to his home. She outranked all of her people but one, the High Priestess of the Dienobolos.

Gods save him.

She was a queen in her own right, and she'd bowed before Kit.

His father likely posed little threat to her, and yet could not see beyond her sex to the threat she posed him, the safety her presence ensured.

"Of course, your majesty." She inclined her head, turning finally to look upon the king while guards hefted the dead and the injured from the field of battle.

Kit's gaze caught hers for a moment, noted the calm glint of her eye, the widened pupil as though she were hiding emotion behind the blank face. These were not her people. A part of him was comforted thinking that perhaps she did not revel in the spilling of unnecessary blood despite her occupation, her past.

"Most qualified or not—"

"Captain." The king turned to stare at Kit's interjection. "She is the captain of my guard, Father. Qualified, trusted, or not, she deserves the respect the position demands."

"She has not earned it in my estimation."

"She has in mine, and as I am your heir. I would hope my word carries some weight with you."

"Kit," the king sighed, shaking his head before looking back at Eli standing patiently before him, quarrel in her hand held unthreateningly at her side now. Leon turned his gaze to Marius. "Ensure that she is relieved from duty before I needs see her in my son's presence. And pray your trust is not misled, for it is all our lives if Kit should die."

Stated so bluntly, Kit blanched.

That his father would state such a truth in the aftermath of so much death was unseemly, threatened to consume Kit with anger, with despair.

"He will not die so long as I am with him, your majesty. I swear it to you, by the Darkness that Rules the Night."

The old man flinched. Kit's uncle and the commander flinched.

It was one thing to know she was from the wood, to discuss belief and magic when fighting for one's life. But that her beliefs were so different, so alien to him and his people, thrown so bluntly into their faces, made Kit flinch, fear what his father's response would be.

"By the will of the Gods, your oath is witnessed."

"And binding."

Kit's gaze went to Marius, the general's solemn face staring at the woman who offered herself to Kit's protection.

By her faith, and his.

Four
One Month Later

I was an assassin, my prince. I killed those who deserved to die, no more. War is a different battleground, but even then, if a life can be spared, the Darkness does not seek to claim it."

She extended her hand, offering aid in rising while he rubbed at his ribs where her sword had struck beneath the shield of his light armor. Trying to kill him or not, she'd found her way around his defenses over and over. That it was part of the exercise did not endear him to the instruction.

Try this. Lift that. Lunge now.

No matter what he attempted, her blades whirled faster, kept him at bay while she struck true.

When he asked what form a particular attack came from, she gave three names, none of which he knew, a hybridization of what she'd learned over her life and adapted to her own style. Of course, she said she was born knowing the ways of death, which he was particularly willing to believe considering how easily she managed to keep him from striking her down.

They'd been at the same exercises for weeks now.

He had bruises on bruises, no time to heal from one bout to another, forced by his father, by her, to practice daily without fail, more if court sessions were short and his schedule allowed.

He didn't dare point out that there had been no subsequent attacks on his person, or that there were no current rumors of attack or threat to the same. Rumors were often silent, and Kit so rarely left the safety of the city walls, he wouldn't know of any planned attacks or not.

The king commanded, and Kit's elfin assassin was surprisingly willing to obey the orders she received to keep him in the lists longer and longer.

"You hesitate on the attack, your highness. Rather than raising your blade to kill, you raise it to practice." She shifted position until she was at his back, her arms wrapping round his waist, cupping his forearms for her lesser height did not allow her to reach his wrists. "Your arms are too tense, too focused on maintaining your form rather than anticipating the strike, defending against it, lunging in turn. You move like one of your knights, strict, straight, unbending; but the monks of Rao Shar could slip between your arms like a lover moving to embrace and you'd find a knife between your ribs before you recognized the danger. They flow like dancers around your rock formations."

"Which means nothing since I am not facing the monks of Rao Shar or the demons of Quiofol or the Forgotten Peoples of Miest or any other person out there beyond the borders of my country!" He tried to pull out of her arms, but her hands only tightened further while he fumed.

Her hands lifted his arms in a parody of the water form she'd shown him the day before, long slashes that rolled like waves against a sea shore, an advance and retreat in one. Yes, the patterns were distinguishable, could be anticipated when made the same each time, but no wave struck the shore twice identically. Her response hadn't stopped him from trying to prove her wrong, flowing through the motions with his broad sword while she danced on the crests out of reach. "It means that your fighting style is too narrow, my prince. And you are not facing them *yet*. They will come if they are hired. Assassins have no creed but that of the orders they accept."

"You said not every attack must be to kill."

"But every attack must be ready to kill." She released his arms, letting him maintain his strict pose or drop his guard at will.

The sword was not meant for the fluid motions of the Rao Shar.

He let his blade point towards the ground and turned to face her.

"We'll start with my people. The Dienobolos fight with short knives, personal, close. It leaves your longer swords at a disadvantage when your opponent is skin to skin and your blade too long to turn on them."

"My sword allows greater reach to keep you from drawing that close in the first place."

"Not if I am fast enough to duck beneath your arm and close upon you before you can respond in kind."

And she was fast enough. How many times had she proved that point over the past month?

He refused to admit she was correct. She was, but he didn't want to feed the lack of ego she already employed. The woman knew her strengths, didn't flinch from them or preen over them. She simply was and while Kit admired it from a military and scholarly standpoint, the swordsman in him resented being constantly beaten back. "Then what do you suggest?"

"If you refuse to learn other weapons than that long sword you wield, then you had better be faster than all your opponents. If you're not fast, then learn blades that can protect you against those who are, the stratagems and movements ingrained in your being so that it is instinct to defend and attack, not thought."

"You said instinct wasn't enough."

"Practice leads to instinct. Once muscle memory takes control of your actions, then instinct is what you can rely on. That allows for a thorough defense." She weaved, her daggers close to her body, nearly pressing them to her chest as she spun around him, her knives arcing so quickly that he missed the lift and draw of them but knew what the motion should be from having practiced it so many times now. The sword was unwieldy when compared to her movements.

Her forms added protection to her person while being deadly against her foes. "I'll show you patterns for knives, long staves, hands. Subtle ways to kill and brutal ways to defend. I've watched enough. I know what you can do and what I can teach you to do if you'll let me."

"I thought you were already teaching me?"

"This was testing. Now the training begins."

He watched her clean the steel of her blade against her slacks.

The silver glinted in the afternoon light, shining along the edge of the weapon. He reached towards that glare, pressed the tip of his finger to the blade, felt the razor sharpness of it against his flesh. A hiss slipped past his lips and he sucked his bloodied digit into his mouth, glaring at his new trainer who was using edged blades against him in practice.

He should be dead one hundred times over.

That she hadn't killed him with her knives was impressive of her skill, and depressing that her skill was what had kept him this side of the void.

Her lips quirked when she noticed him glaring at her. "A spell, Prince, to blunt the edges for practice but that obeys my will when the blade needs to be used in defense."

"It saves you from having to sharpen the metal daily."

"It saves me from ever being unarmed, even when the weapon is perceived harmless."

She spun the hilts of her knives in her palms, catching the weapon by the handle when the blade pointed away from her body, an impressive display of timing and skill.

Kit found the motions hypnotizing, unable to look away from the twirl and catch before him. Other soldiers were in the practice square. Distantly he was aware of the clang of steel against steel, had known that he was not alone though likely the only one getting his ass handed to him routinely. But the knowledge did nothing to distract him from the woman before him, or more precisely, from letting the motions of her knives lull him into a near daze, his exhaustion making its untimely appearance. The thought of returning to the lists for another round made his chest ache like a boy about to lift a sword for the first time, remembered terror and pained future exertion.

"Not tonight, Highness. A few days perhaps, to recover, before we begin again?"

He shook his head, blinked away the dust and sweat in his eyes. What had she said?

Her eyebrows rose, the half-smile lightening into a grin at his lack of comprehension. "Have I worked you that hard, Prince?"

He couldn't help himself. The smile came to his lips without thought at her words, easy to grin at the playfulness in her tone, the lack of biting critique or harsh command. "Gods yes."

She laughed, though he felt her gaze on him, lingering where she had struck him throughout the day, and the days prior.

He met her green stare, watched her lips turn down, felt his face morph to match. "Is everything all right?"

Her head tilted at his question.

He waited for her response, worried that she was going to renege on her offer of a few days of rest.

"You haven't smiled like that since the woods. I thought I'd never see it again."

Heat flamed in his cheeks, likely unnoticed beneath the layer of crime covering him. No one ever seemed to call him on his smile, no one but her. "You're the only one to comment on my expressions."

"No one else realizes that the upturn of your lips is anything but what it's meant to emulate." She took both knives in one hand, extending the other to take his sword from him.

He took her weapons instead, chivalry demanding he at least pretend to treat a lady as a lady even if said lady was deadlier than he.

She followed him over the hard packed sand of the arena towards the barracks, the weapons master who claimed each practice blade, ensured that wet stones and swordsmiths were at the ready if someone needed an edge.

Five men ringed a pair of combatants, soldiers having reverted to wrestling when the sun waned beyond the outer wall of the courtyard. Groups of the same stood along the sentry points, staring out over the city shielded from view by the sandstone built around the palace.

Kit knew the view from atop those walls. The spires of temples reaching into the sky, thatched and shingled roofs, some flat with small awnings atop their backs for residents to escape the crowded streets for a night beneath the stars. How many times had Kit wanted to spend the night atop one of those small homes, staring at the sky rather than stone vaulted ceilings blocking out the night around him. Or looking beyond the city, to the green pastures, yellow corn fields, a patchwork of nature far beyond what he could see, supporting the lives of the men and women who called his country home. The woods too, great trees standing unbent in the distance, their secrets hidden beneath a canopy of leaves.

The days were finally growing warmer, though winter's bite had yet to truly lift in the air. Soon enough warm would turn to heat and then to snow once more.

Her touch on his hand drew him back to the moment, had his fingers tightening on the blades though she held his wrist to stop whatever attack he would have perpetrated.

"Instinct."

He managed a small grin, not forgetting her words from before, not willing to smile in truth, needing to keep the expression to himself lest he forget not to fall under her spell once more.

She handed her knives and his sword to the blacksmith. "I'll need another set, two inches longer, an ounce or two heavier but no more. You'll have to keep the blades proportioned but light."

"Like the steel used for these beauties?" Grizzled hands touched the tang of each blade with care, honoring the weapons, their intent and craftsmanship.

Kit would have found the gesture odd, but the man was an artist even if his craft was warfare. Not that his brain had enough energy to care at the moment.

"Exactly, just like I showed you."

Showed him what? Him? Kit? Or the sword master? What were they talking about?

"And who are the blades for, my lady?"

"The prince."

"Now wait a moment—"

She turned to meet Kit's gaze, brows raised at his stuttered complaint, and he tried to recall the train of the conversation he'd heard but not been listening too.

Her arms crossed over her chest in silent reprimand to his inattention.

How did she do that?

She was, technically speaking, his servant, in a way, and yet with a single look, he held his tongue, bowing to her will. He should be furious with her that she had so much power over him. Fine, yes, alright, he could recognize the authority of another leader. But just because he recognized it didn't mean he should obey. And yes, he'd admit to a small amount of jealousy that she wielded such authority so easily where it sat without much weight on his shoulders.

Kit blamed the last part on the fact that everyone was always tiptoeing around him.

Must protect the prince. The prince cannot be hurt.

Well princes needed to rule and the constant subversion of his rule was weakening him in the eyes of his people since he was surrounded by a contingent of guards or spoke through his father's words, his own never acknowledged.

Anger swelled in his breast. He deserved her respect, the swordsmith's, his soldiers. He was good with a damn blade. He wasn't incompetent despite how she made him appear. He'd survive any battle posed against him. He would, despite what she might think. He was sure that there was someone out their better with a weapon than his elf. There had to be someone out there better than his elf, someone meant for him, who wouldn't run from him after a damn ball because he said he was in love…

The humor in her gaze changed to concern. He forced his fists to relax at his sides, tried to coral his expression into something benign.

He wasn't this type of person. He was calm, even tempered. Nothing riled him and yet around her, nothing was normal or sane. He was letting the damn pit in his stomach disrupt his life, those strange flutters in the vicinity of his chest anytime she came near distract him, tie him up in knots. It was so easy to say he wasn't going to give in to her, wasn't going to feel anything for her, and something very different to live with the results. Easier to change a river's path than the way she made him feel, look in her eyes and see a complete lack of reciprocation in them.

That was it, wasn't it? That she didn't feel for him the way he felt for her.

He blinked, met that upraised stare. "What do I need daggers for?"

"To learn to fight with."

"And the practice daggers we already have?"

"The way your weapons are formed are different than my peoples. To fight like my brethren, you will need weapons like them. If you find that your style adapts to using your knives with more efficacy than mine, then you're welcome to use your own blades. But as I am your instructor, you will learn my way, and only when I deem you proficient will your considerations be taken into account."

"And that I am prince?"

"Means nothing when it is your defense we are discussing."

She was uncompromising.

Why that helped steady him, he didn't know.

It wasn't just her expertise with a blade he could learn from her, this woman who pushed emotion aside to focus on the need at hand. She made a good instructor, had been renowned as the best of assassins, the head of her guild, if elves formed into guilds. She'd make a wise tactician and general someday, if those skills were required. He could allow himself to admire those qualities in her. A safe way to deny his emotions, accepting a few to bury the others beneath.

He looked at the blacksmith. "How long until the blades can be forged?"

"A week, Prince."

"You're not to deny your other duties to make those weapons. We'll make do with what we have until they're ready. Is that understood?"

"Of course, your highness."

He nodded at the man. "Is that sufficient for your requirements, Captain?"

"Quite, my prince."

"Then are we finished for today?"

She nodded, and he returned the gesture before walking away, needing to walk away.

As expected, he felt her presence at his back, her shadow stretching towards his in the late waning sunlight.

He paused at the door of her rooms.

She did not enter.

"I am going to my rooms, Captain. There are guards on my door, likely one on my balcony. There are no state dinners for tonight, nothing to fear or worry over. A meal with the king, and then bed. I don't need a shadow in my own palace."

"If you think that then you need one all the more."

"Not tonight." He didn't mean for the edge in his voice to cut her, the small flinch he wouldn't have seen if he hadn't been watching her so closely. She'd made a vow to the king. That was why she was so adamant about keeping him in her care. There was nothing else in her gaze but duty, and he would do well to remember that. "You're relived for the evening, Captain. If you're resolute on having me watched, set someone else to the task, but I'd not have your shadow after mine tonight."

He wanted solitude, for just a moment, he wanted solitude. He wanted to be far from her and whatever it was she made him feel.

"As you will, my prince."

His eyes closed in silent gratitude, and she turned towards her rooms, the sound of her boots loud on the crunching sands of the training grounds, the thunk of her door closing when she left him alone.

He retreated to the palace and to his chambers, a bath drawn and ready for him, his steward urging him out of his soiled clothing and into the heated water the moment Kit opened the door.

Not right away though. He let the servant undress him, take his clothing, ask if there was anything else Kit required before leaving the prince to his bath.

Kit leaned against the sink, eyes closed, preparing himself for a lonely meal with his father, the less awkward drinks in the library that would follow, the formalities over with for the evening. He loved the old man, but his father was king, and his mother had been the love of his father's life. Kit looked too much like his dam to ease the man's heartache, and it was only with alcohol in the king's system that Kit felt truly accepted by the man who'd sired him.

With a groan, he lowered himself into the steaming water, letting the heat soak into his abused muscles, the bruises decorating his chest and back, his arms and legs. Just a few moments rest before the emotionally grueling dinner.

At least he had the day off the practice field tomorrow.

He wondered how long it would take before Marius heard that the captain had planned a brief stay of degradation on the arena floor and came to train Kit himself.

Ah to sink beneath the bath water and hold his breath.

He stood and resigned himself to duty, hardened his heart with the word.

Chapter III
One

He was sitting in the library, alone now that the bells had chimed fourth hour of the new day, the king finally retreating to his own rooms and leaving his son in peace.

She watched him from the corner. The way his hand cradled his chin, his eyes fluttering closed before he jerked awake.

One month.

Sweet Darkness, she'd been here for a month already, one month of sparring, of training, of doing her best not to see the man beyond the soldier's blade she tutored, the solemn face that rarely smiled in her presence.

No, that wasn't really what was worrying her. What worried her was that she'd been here for only a month, and she no longer thought of the woods of her birth as her home. Not that she thought of the walls as her home either, just that, staring at the prince, she found a peace she'd not felt surrounded by her own people, worshipping her own faith, performing her ascribed duties. With him, with him she found herself.

She'd never shied from killing.

She was what the Darkness had made her and she wasn't ashamed of the part of her soul that was violent, that was sure, that was a killer, a justice dealer, mercy for the suffering and death for the wicked. There had been no times where she took a life undeserved, where she slayed without reason or cause.

She was, and that had been enough for her until they danced the waltz and she found that she rather enjoyed the way someone else looked at her, liked knowing that he saw something beyond the First of Assassins, beyond the bleakness of her path in life. He'd seen a woman, and she wished desperately that she was still that person to him.

She blinked, met his stare, his body no longer relaxing to sleep where he sat in his chair, one hand at his hip and the dagger she knew he kept there at her insistence.

He didn't drop his gaze, waiting for her to do or say or make excuses as to why she'd disobeyed his order for peace and intruded upon it.

She willed her fingers to relax at her side. Concerns she hadn't felt since before she accepted the Darkness made her stomach turn when she looked at him, that strange tingling in her nerves that failed to flee whenever she was in his presence. "I would like to request to be relieved of guard duty for the next three evenings."

Surely he'd grant the request. She'd relieved him of training for the same allotment of time. Quid pro quo and the like.

His eyes narrowed, focusing on her in the darkness, searching her face for what she didn't know.

She was grateful to be standing in the shadows to hide her blush from his piercing gaze.

"Why?"

Why indeed.

How much to tell him? What amount would see him grant the request without him asking for more than her faith allowed her to give? The Dark of the Moon were sacred days to her people. There were rituals to perform, offerings to make, sacrifices to endure, rest to take. "It's a religious obligation."

"And you'll return to the woods? To the people who you killed for my life?"

"No."

He must have heard the edge to her words, wondered at it. He must have, yet he did not question her further. That he didn't made her anger rise, but that rising emotion implied a longing for more than she was willing to give him. She should appreciate his circumspection. But that he didn't ask inferred a lack of caring and Darkness take it, she wanted him to care, to maintain that damnable need for her he'd had when he asked her to stay, before he knew who she truly was, when she was simply Ella and he was Kit and prince and assassin didn't matter.

"Will this ritual entail the harming of any of my countrymen?" He asked the question neutrally, eyes holding hers though she saw no emotion in their depths.

"No."

"Will the obligation damage my land or my people's homes?"

"No."

"Will the evenings be enough for you to complete whatever it is you're doing, or do you require the whole day?"

"It's—" She would have laughed at his ability to ask without asking what she was doing, but she held her tongue. The first two questions cared for his county. The last cared for her. "It must be performed at the darkest hour."

He stood from his chair, hands at the small of his back. He crossed to the fire burning merrily behind the grate in the library wall. She watched his profile, the expressionless mask over his face, the flickering flames that hid the emotion in his eyes.

"We have holy days too, you know. Days of commitment that we hold sacred." His head turned, and she crossed the room to stand at his side, letting him look at her now as she stared into the fire, into the light. "Did you think you needed to bribe me with a few days free of training to grant your request?"

"No," she paused, "but I did not think it would hurt any."

"Would you tell me about it, if I asked?"

That he didn't command soothed her even while her heartbeat sped at the interest the question implied. "None of your people have ever witnessed our rituals."

"I did not ask to witness, Captain."

She shifted, turning to face him, waiting until he did the same for her. She couldn't help herself from reaching up and pressing his strands of midnight hair behind his ear. His eyes widened at the gesture, the pupils expanding at the highly inappropriate touch given who they were and where they were, but he didn't stop her, and she let her fingers linger in his tangled curls, glance over the cords of his neck, his shoulders before slipping back to her side. Her pulse raced. His gaze dipped to the beat in her throat, quickly back to her eyes. "I cannot explain it other than for you to see."

"And is it the type of ritual outsiders are allowed to share in?"

You're not an outsider.

The words were there on her lips, ready to leap into the air between them. She had to bite her tongue to hold the avowal back. "I don't know. Not many visitors entered the Woods, and none who did asked to witness what it was to be a Child of the Night. But the Darkness touches all, even those believing in younger gods. The Night will not rebuke any who choose to reside in Its glory."

"Yet you live in the day."

"Yes."

Whether he shifted or she did, she couldn't say, only that it was no longer the fire that seared heat into her flesh, and if not for the clench of her hands at her sides, fingers buried in the folds of her slacks, for the grasp of his hands behind his back, she would have wrapped herself around him, uncaring that she refused his emotions and he played cool towards her.

"It would be an honor then, to be welcomed to witness your faith."

"So that you can learn yet more of my people?"

He blinked, and she watched him accept her offered respite from the intimacy of the moment. "Yes, a chance to learn more of your people."

She heard: more of you. "I would use the glade, at the far edges of the gardens then."

"A wise choice, beyond the normal prying eyes of the court."

"Yes."

He nodded, and the gesture brought his lips a breath away from hers, only a small rise on her toes, and the choice between them would be gone. She knew he waited for her choice, knew that if she reached those final inches between them, he would not let her go back to being his captain, and she would not want to, and it was too soon. Much too soon to be playing games with the rest of their lives. He was not safe. His life was not his own, not until his five hundredth and something birthday.

He needed a captain, someone who could be reason and violence, who would protect him even from himself, and if she kissed him now, despite the odd flutter in her heart at the thought, he would put her life before his, and damn the Night because she wanted that and had too great a sense of duty to allow him to make such a sacrifice.

She stepped away and his head snapped back, the brief play of emotion in his eyes dimmed to its familiar indifference.

"I will leave at sunset tomorrow."

"I will inform Marius of your absence."

She hesitated, hearing the dismissal in his voice and debating the sanity of pushing, staying, any longer. "It is a monthly observance," she nearly said his name, nickname. She offered his title instead, "My Prince."

"I will inform the General to make considerations as such."

"Thank you, my lord."

He continued to stare at her, and she fought the urge to twitch. Her, the greatest assassin of the Dienobolos, fidgeting before a prince of the city.

"Captain."

She nodded, gave him her back, and left him to his silence in the library.

The door closed behind her, and she forced herself not to turn around, walk back into the room she'd left, beg for forgiveness for the distance needed between them.

Instead, she fled through the palace walls, to the courtyard beyond and her rooms, hiding in her small sanctuary, away from her prince and the burning desire for him that wouldn't abate.

Two

S he waited for the sun to set in her bedroom, watching the last lingering rays of daylight fade into the western sky. Twilight bloomed over the horizon in a bevy of reds and oranges, faded to blue and azure, stars twinkling at the edges of the darkness.

The red bag she found in the pantry sat beside her door.

A stick of incense scented with lilies to honor Pirie, the aspect of the Dark to whom prayers were offered. Seven seeds, two from a peach, one from a rose, four from the grain grown in rows beyond the edges of the walled city, to honor Rouchim, Lady of the Earth, the Giver. She bought a toy boat in the shops near the port one afternoon, a gift to Ashet, the Builder, for the home Eli lived in, be it wood or stone. Her blood she carried within her, a gift to Liaea, to nourish the earth where the body lived upon its death, where all things came from before their birth. There was a knife in her bag, ceremonial and sharp, to honor the flesh and the darkness that filled it.

For Echi there was pain.

She was a servant of Justice, even stripped of the title. Her soul was bound to the Judge of the Night.

She had taken four lives unsanctioned by her people to save one not of her own. She could argue that since she was the highest of her order, her taking of the lives was sanctioned and deserved no recompense, but she was not afraid of paying the debt.

Her eyes scanned the bulge of the martinet in her bag, the flogger handed down through generations, held by the hands of the Elichisolos before her, should be held by those who followed in her stead. She'd spilled her blood by the weapon in the past, once for every time her soul needed purging. Never before had shame filled her at the need to touch the weapon.

It was sacrifice.

The Darkness demanded it.

In her soul, the deepest, blackest parts of it, where her connection to the Night pulsed strong and true, she held no regret, held no sorrow at her actions in saving the prince.

But justice was demanded.

She would abide by tradition, especially here, where her traditions were unknown, subverted, ignored.

She was not ashamed of the demands of her faith.

She donned her cloak, pulling the hood over her head, hiding her auburn hair beneath the deep blue velvet. The bag she slung over her shoulder, settling it against her side.

A patrol marched past her door, and she slipped out at the passing. Her feet found the path around the castle and to the gardens beyond.

She padded over the stone paths, walked into the darkness without a torch to guide her way.

She had not sought him out during the day, neither rescinding nor reminding him of her offer the night before. A part of her hoped that he would not be there, in the glade, when she reached the area. Another part hoped he would, for she had never been alone for the Offering, and she was so alone here in the city, separated from the ones who knew her, and the ones who would have worshipped as she did, even if they were not familiar with her person.

He wouldn't understand the rituals involved in the service. He had too much honor to understand beating anyone, let alone self-inflicted penance.

It wasn't something she had to worry about yet though.

It wasn't something she was likely to have to worry about regardless.

She stepped onto the cool spring grass, the earth cold, only the barest hint of summer in the air. The first spring blossoms were beginning to bloom. Shoots of green rising after a winter buried beneath the snow. A mild winter, considering. They'd not had more than a few feet of white, not in the woods and not without them.

The earth was dry.

Rain would be a blessing so long as it did not turn to sleet.

Perhaps she would add that to her list of prayers.

She entered the grove, the trees surrounding the small fountain built for lover's trysts within the woods. Not that the denizens of Tornald would engage in such physical exertions, not with their taboo on a simple kiss.

Eli slipped the bag from her shoulder, knelt to lay out the contents on the ground. She stripped the cloak from her shoulder, layering the earth with the velvet for her offerings to rest on.

Naked as the day she came into the world, she genuflected with her hands folded in her lap, head tilted back to the sky, the cold of the late night raising goose pimples on her skin. She waited for the witching hour to come, whispering the silent prayers of her people to the wood.

She opened her eyes to the darkness, her magic mingling with the night around her, wrapping her in shadows, cradling her in its embrace.

With a flick of her fingers, she lit a flame at the end of the stick of incense, letting the sweet scent of flowers fill the small grove, cast a hazy fog within the Shadow.

Her fingers found the offerings easily enough. There was no fumbling when she lifted the seeds in her hands, cupped them to her lips and blew. Black tendrils of shadow rose to enfold the little stones in their embrace, sinking into the hard shells of the pips, seeking out the essence of life held within each tiny bulb.

The seeds turned to hard gems, the offering accepted and remembered by the Darkness.

It took only a thought to pass the gems through the cloth covering the ground, burying the offering within the winter firm earth, something to wait on the warmth of summer to grow.

The small boat sailed along on a wave of Night, flowed over the air around her, towards the fountain in the center of the clearing, set to float along the gently rippling water, buoyed there despite the chunks of ice dotting the basin.

Eli watched the boat disappear around the edge of the mermaid rising in the center of the pool. Her people were not seafarers. She'd never set foot on a boat and doubted she ever would. If they fished, it was at the edges of the lakes and ponds throughout the forest. But there was something beautiful about the waves. She'd listened to them beating the shore late at night at the edge of the city. The rhythmic rush and fall of sand roiling soothed her like the sound of wind through leaves.

She lifted the knife, pressed her lips to the blade beneath the hilt, offering a silent prayer to the glinting blade in the darkness, shining despite the lack of light around it. Her free hand opened, palm flat in the air before her. Economical, she pierced the center of her hand with the knife, opening her skin until a pool of blood formed. She cut over the length of scar from the sword stained with Beracsh's blood.

She replaced the dagger on her cloak.

Her predecessor, the Elichisolos who ruled before Eli offered herself to the Darkness, had chosen the cougar for his sigil, the cat an elegant creature, strong and sure in its presence. Before him came the wolf, a man who believed in pack, who held the woods against the city dwellers, the trolls and the dwarves, the demons from Quiofol and the dragons of the sleeping lands.

When offered the position, she took the emblem of the fox. Quick and agile as the cougar, proud and strong as the wolf, all with the cunning of the hunter and the terror of the prey. The fox knew both sides of the stalking ground, something humans too often forgot in their own arrogance.

She dipped her fingers in the pool of blood in her hand, traced the outline of the fox branded into the skin on the right side of her pelvis, shivering in the chill when the cold air dried the blood on her flesh.

The marking complete, she clenched her bloodied hand into a fist, leaned over her cloak to ensure that five drops of red fell on hard packed earth.

With the last drop, the wound on her palm healed, a black swath of night wrapping her hand for a moment before disappearing, taking the last of her sacrifice with it, carried on the wind to join with the offerings of the rest of her brethren.

The Priestosolos would gather the offerings of the elves within the great Mother Tree this night. She would commit the gifts of blood and grain and wood to the temple altar, allowing the Darkness to claim the devotions of the children of the wood.

Eli had never seen the ceremony. She was not a priest and her only experience within Eao, the Great Temple, had been when she offered herself to Echi and been accepted as the Blade of the Darkness.

If she'd been invited to see the inner sanctum as a child at her mother's heels, she didn't remember it. The Priestosolos had never been comfortable with Eli after the offering ceremony. She and her mother, one executioner, one healer, could not see eye to eye, though the High Priestess had taught Eli much over the years. They'd never been close as family. Eli had no connection beyond blood between her birth mother and birth father, each honored for their place in the tribe, as Eli was, had been, honored, their teachings respected as elder law.

She opened her eyes, watched the last of the darkness clear around her until she knelt in the dim light of the stars, bare to the Night.

She was a servant of Echi, not her mother, no longer the woods.

Echi demanded that penance be given in the open, exposed to the world as it was meant to be naked to the soul in judgment and salvation.

Her tongue formed the words of her people, head bowed in supplication, in atonement. "I do not know my purpose. I have failed You as I was meant to be and flounder as I now am. I beg guidance. I beg forgiveness. I offer my suffering so You would know my sincerity and grant Your wisdom on Your child."

"The Darkness does not listen to outcasts."

She looked into the shadows between the trees, watched five of her once brethren emerge, dressed in black cloths, swathed from head to toe so that only their eyes were visible to the Night. "You would kill me on our sacred day?"

"Kill you?" The woman was smaller than her companions though the men with her yielded to her words. "No, we would not kill you. We seek only the justice of Echi against one of the Dark's own."

"I have committed no crime against Echi. I am the Judgment of our people."

"The prince's life was forfeit long before you took the position."

"I am the Judgment. I decide whose life is forfeit and whose life is sacrosanct."

"At the cost of your brethren's lives?"

"They knew the cost of attacking their Elichisolos."

"Yet you did not return. You did not announce their sin but ran away. Your actions find fault in yourself, not the dead."

Eli blinked, stood. She did not take her gaze from the woman, even as the men flooded the grove to surround her. "I accept my exile. I have not stepped foot within the woods. I honor our traditions."

"You defame them with this farce we have witnessed this day."

She did not argue that her offerings had been accepted by the Darkness. The truth would bring no peace to these elves surrounding her. "What would you have of me then?"

"Penance."

Eli didn't expect the strike of the whip, nor the skill with which it was wielded.

The cord wrapped around her wrist, pulling her off balance while a second struck her opposite side, laying open a line of fire along her flesh.

Echi demanded three times repayment the suffering caused.

Four lives were at her feet. Twelve strikes to balance the scales.

She didn't fight the lashes landing against her skin, from the accidental strikes that lacked strength, to the ones that broke flesh and drew blood to the surface.

"Nine."

The female unleashed the whips at her hips, taking the handles of each in hand, uncoiling the twin tails on the ground before her.

"Ten."

Eli ducked her head, squeezing her eyes closed when the lashes cut across her cheeks and chest, drew blood from the barb tipped tails. Her knees buckled. She barely caught herself on her hands, fighting nausea now that she counted the offering complete.

The woman drew back her metal tipped whip, letting the left fly once more towards Eli's face.

With her hands pressing into the dirt, her knees on the bloodied remains of her cloak, Eli called the Darkness around her, a final offering to be accepted or denied. The whip came closer. Eli watched the barbs' approach.

A wave of midnight surged around her, enclosing her in a shield of ebony, accepted and protected by the faith she worshipped. She touched her hands to the miasma, laughed at the gentle thrum of power seeping beneath her skin. The Darkness surged through her veins healing welt and reel, clothing her in its armor against her once brethren, betraying the condemnation of their beliefs.

Starlight flickered into the glade, pierced the shell around her.

The Darkness faded, left her protected in its warmth to face the men and woman.

"The penance was twelve strikes. The Darkness accepted my offering. I am still Its child. You have betrayed Its teachings for vengeance sake."

The woman snarled, drew back her whip for another strike, no pretense of penance in her attack.

Eli growled.

She was faster than the strike of a whip. Had she chosen, she could have dodged each blow landed against her. But she had owed the suffering to the Darkness, had paid the debt willingly, letting the lives of her people be the penance for leaving the fold of the faith and home to be with her prince, so far beyond the Darkness' reach. This was not the same. This was battle. She was not of the forest any longer. She'd made her offering and it was accepted. The holiness of the day acknowledged and the ceremony complete. She broke no laws in fighting those who would attack her now.

The whip with its barbed tail curled around her wrist, dug into her flesh.

She twisted her arm, yanking the handle from the woman, pulling the whip to her own use, her speed making the others step away from her attack.

"I am not of the Dienobolos any longer. I am foresworn, outcast. I am allowed to defend myself even against my once kin." She smiled at the men around her, baring her teeth in a sneer, ignoring the woman struggling back to her feet. "If I kill you all, I suffer no greater penalty than that which my soul feels at killing those who would kill me."

"You are exiled for four hundred years—"

"Yes." She stared at the men. "But I can kill you with impunity because of it." The snarl faded from her lips, sadness at the unnecessary loss of life replaced the cold emotion in her eyes. "Do not make me."

It was not a plea, and yet it was.

The choice was on their heads.

One of the men nodded, wound his whip around his arm, the others following his example.

Her blood dripped at her side, the barbed tail embedded in the flesh of her wrist, ignored until the threat faded.

The elves stepped back into the woods, back into the garden to make the climb over the wall that surrounded it, return to the wild forests of their homeland.

Eli pulled the barbs from her wrist, coiling the whip, her concession from the woman who would have broken the laws of their people. She watched the female stand. The elf's arm drew back and Eli heard the broken step of a booted foot sliding to a halt to her left.

She was quicker on the throw, more accurate, her commandeered whip wrapped in jagged lines around the woman's throat, tearing gouges into the flesh.

Kit hissed, but it was the stranger who died, the wicked metal barbs having pierced the thin covering of cloth and skin and nicking an artery in the woman's throat.

The fresh scent of iron tinged the air.

Eli watched the black cloth darken with spilled blood.

His sword rang from his scabbard. He moved to flank her at her right, giving her the dominant position though she doubted he realized that's what he did.

He did not ask if this was part of the ritual.

She did not offer an explanation as the woman gasped her last, clutching at her throat, spasms racking the dying body before going motionless on the ground.

He tensed when shadows filled the trees, spilled out on the ground, hiding the glade in its dark embrace. She caught the tightening of his shoulders from the corner of her eye, the way he shifted onto the balls of his feet, preparing to meet whatever attack was coming. His sword disappeared within the shade, nothing to defend against, held steady though he did not swing.

Her gaze strayed to the darkened tree line, the black clad eyes staring out at her from within the first blossoming of leaves.

She blinked, and the darkness cleared, the body gone from the ground between elf and wood.

"Will they return?" His voice was steady, his arms unshaking at her side, eyes roving the tree line, not trusting her brethren's retreat.

"No." Her lids closed, heart steadying now that the threat was passed, both to her and to her prince. "The attack was unprovoked. They'll return the woman to the forest, but she betrayed her faith by intending to kill on this night."

"You killed."

"To defend my own life. To defend yours. My actions were just, Kit. Hers were not."

He sheathed his blade.

His eyes went to her body, trailed down the shadow silk armor covering her, the metal plates a harder substance than any steel he could touch, lighter than air.

She had not expected him to take her arm, flinched when his hand rose to hers. He didn't pull away, keeping his grip on her bicep while turning her hand towards him, looking at the blood seeping down her wrist from the slice of the whip she'd stolen.

He was bloodied too, a rent in his shirt showing a growing stain of red from where the woman's whip had struck.

Eli'd not been quick enough to spare him any injury.

"But you spared my life."

She pressed her free hand to his chest, staring into his steel gray eyes, knowing that hers were eerie, at best, when she called the darkness to her. He didn't flinch away, not when she felt the flickering of her pupils, or when strands of shadow magic uncurled from her fingers and eased into his wound, mending torn flesh, leaving only a scar in its stead.

He cupped her cheek, his thumb brushing the ridge below her eye, brushing until the magic faded. "You didn't heal yourself."

She looked at her seeping wrist. "Penance, for the life I took to save ours."

"You said it was just."

"Just" didn't mean guiltless.

He didn't press further.

Her cloak, the incense, the seeds and boat, all of it was consumed by the Darkness. All of it gone but for the ceremonial dagger glinting in the pale star light. She caught her breath when he bent to retrieve it, lifting it carefully from its cradle of grass, handing it to her with the reverence ritual required.

"Thank you."

He nodded.

She slipped the knife into a pocket of the flowing shadows clothing her. He extended his arm and she wrapped hers within his embrace, letting him lead her from the grove. Her bare feet made no sound on the cold stone, too used to moving quietly on any surface regardless of shoes or not. He matched her, silencing his steps best he could. She said nothing for his efforts, though she smiled at his attempt. He'd grow silent under her tutelage soon enough, but he was not training to be an assassin, and sometimes a stampede succeeded in instilling fear where silence did not.

Three

He led her to the palace, ignoring the turn to the barracks and taking her into the lower level of the great castle, to the rooms she'd not yet explored.

His hold on her arm tightened as he helped her down the stairs to the servant's quarters and military council area. She'd heard of the rooms, if not been there. He was solicitous, though she didn't need the aid in walking, enjoying his touch all the same. "The baths," he nodded to his right at a wide door from which heat seeped. There was no sign to the room, but it would have been easy enough to deduce what loomed behind the doors based on the sound of running water coming from within.

She used her private bath.

But it was good to know the location, even if he'd told her, obliquely, that first day where the public washrooms were.

He pointed with his free hand, directing her gaze to the far end of the hall bathed in darkness, rare torches lighting the way at this hour of the night. "The healer is at the end there, his rooms taking up the southern wing of the palace with the healing ward. He's some skill with magic, not like you, but something similar when it comes to the healing of the flesh, though he prefers not to use it, I think." He didn't elaborate, and she nodded like she understood.

Of course, she probably did understand better than he. For some people, their magic was finite in its strength and power. There were other means of healing someone if the wound wasn't severe enough to merit calling on enchantments deep within.

Her eyes turned up to his, meeting the gaze he leveled at her, his steps slow and steady while they walked down the hall. "Is allowing him to look at your wrist against your customs?"

The question was unexpected and she stopped, pulling him to a halt beside her.

She liked the caring it implied, for her, for her faith.

"No, I do not need to see him; and no, it is not against my beliefs to have the wound attended to by another healer. But I am a Daughter of Echi."

"Your god of justice."

"The Aspect of the Darkness that deals in Justice." She watched his brows knit over his forehead, lips open to argue semantics with her, close.

The Darkness was. It was not a being like his gods. She'd tried to explain it before, but failed. It was why she was a servant of the Night, and not a priest in the temple.

"I tend my own wounds when I can."

He took the out she offered, not arguing theology with her, though she knew it was not an argument he sought, just knowledge. "Very well."

He drew her forward, continuing on, leading her the Darkness knew where.

The door he opened had a frosted glass window, the wood warped so that it bulged towards the hall even though it swung forward into the space it guarded. Coals burned merrily in a grate in one corner of the wood paneled room. Despite the obvious upkeep, she had the impression the chamber was seldom used.

He ushered her into the space, closing the door behind them.

Two tables sat in the center of the area, cushioned to lie upon though the reason why someone would choose to sleep here rather than their own beds was beyond her. But she was not a prince, not hunted by assassins and guards every minute of the day. This well could be a place of peace for him.

"Do you even realize that you are shaking?"

His arm no longer linked through hers, instead curving about her waist, holding her to his side while she took in the small area. And it was small, yet she felt like she'd yet to see the whole of it.

Her gaze snapped to his, but the motion took an eternity to complete. She'd felt the shaking, yes, but had thought it was from him, ignored the odd lethargy suffusing her limbs.

It wasn't poison. Her body would have fought against poison, warned her if that was what was attacking her system.

Her hand shook when she raised it to her forehead to wipe the sweat from her brow.

He sat her on a table, and it was the most natural thing to allow him to step between her legs so that his arms could remain wrapped around her, supporting her. "Was your wrist the only injury tonight?"

Her head tipped to the side, eyes blinking rapidly up at him.

He would not like to know that she had been whipped, or that she'd been planning on whipping herself.

She raised her hand, brushing back the stubborn lock of hair that was always falling over his eye. So black, his hair, like the Darkness in her eyes when she called magic to her. The smears of red on his skin looked wrong. She tried to brush the blood away but it smeared further. A small yelp escaped her lips when he pulled away and swung her legs onto the table, laid her down before standing at her side, looking down at her wrist in his hand.

The shadow silk was slick through with her blood. It stung when he peeled the fabric away from her flesh, revealed the marks where the barbs broke her skin.

"Damnit, Ella." His fingers clamped on her arm, squeezing her hand to his chest.

She should pull away.

She meant to, but his grip was too strong and she liked the way he held her to keep her close, keep her present.

Her eyes blinked open, his lips moving but the words were distant. "Come on sweetheart. Heal the wound, Ella. Call the darkness and heal yourself."

It was the Darkness, not darkness. She wanted to tell him that, but he looked so worried that she decided that discussion could wait for later.

She closed her eyes, his free hand shaking her shoulder, jostling her awake once more.

"Don't fall asleep. Stay with me."

"I'm calling my magic. It hurts to concentrate."

His mere presence was distraction, but she managed to pierce the veil, call the otherworldly Obsidian to her will, force her flesh to heal, seal the arteries and veins beneath, encourage her blood to replenish and flow throughout her body once more. The last calmed the rasping of her breath, eased the tension in her chest. Her eyes focused on the scars, the faint lines visible between the grip of his fingers.

The woman had nicked an artery, multiple times, it appeared.

Eli hadn't realized the severity of the wound.

She might have survived it, even without treating the injury, if the Darkness was merciful. Likely she would have remained at her vigil in the glade and passed into the night without anyone the wiser.

Her gaze focused back on him, noting the intensity of his return stare, the way his fingers brushed against her skin in a gentler caress now that the wound was healed.

"Thank you."

"For what?" The gruffness of his voice had her fighting a smile, a blush at the way his gaze pierced her.

"For saving my life."

"I didn't do anything, Captain."

"You recognized that something needed to be done. I wouldn't have realized until too late."

He smiled down at her before flinching and backing away, letting her hand drop to the mattress, separating them now that the immediate threat was annulled. "Only thrice more and we're even then."

"Are you keeping score?"

He didn't respond.

Her body was weak, but she forced herself to sit all the same, hands braced on the sides of the bed as she stared around herself at the room she was in, better able to examine it now that her mind wasn't muddled with imminent demise. Her lips quirked with the thought, quickly stilled and willed away. "What is this place?"

He looked away when her gaze landed on him though his eyes flicked back towards her though he tried not to stare. "A sauna. My great something or other grandfather had it installed for his wife. Apparently the lady was from Wen and enjoyed the balmy island climate there, ours too cold for her."

"The lady? Don't you know her name?" Eli grinned at the question, hoping it would put him at ease, annul the tension between them.

"She left soon after her arrival here. She's not even in our history books."

"A harsh fate."

He looked back at her, one hand resting behind him to lean against the table opposite hers. "Yes. But she was unhappy, and Grandfather kept her name from our histories so that she might have a chance at a life outside of our realm. Perhaps she found something more to her liking somewhere else."

"That's a compassionate way of looking at a cuckold."

A bark of laughter escaped him, and she smiled at his response. "He wasn't happy with her either. Between the two of them, the only time they spent together was in this room, someplace where silence and rest was appreciated and they didn't need to speak to one another."

There was a wistfulness to his words that she wondered if he heard. "And why do you come to this room, Kit?"

"Because I can be alone here, Captain, and I find it restful."

Yes, she could understand that response, even commiserate with it.

Of course, she found being with the man himself restful.

"I'm sorry I was late to your ceremony. I might have been able to aid you against the elves who attacked had I been on time."

"From my perspective, my prince, your timing was perfect."

He moved from his position on the bed, walked to the coals and ladled a cup of water over the gentle heat from a bucket built into the wall itself. Coils of tubing pierced the grate, allowing for a slow trickle to constantly feed against the heat of the stones, keep steam circulating within the chamber. But the ladle added more fuel to the flame, increased the heat of the temperate room to the inhabitants liking. He seemed to enjoy the added moisture, eyes closing as the steam drifted towards his face.

Her clothing began to stick to her skin, and she was not as thrilled with the result, though said nothing to disrupt him, to ruin this moment between them.

"You will worship again tomorrow and Vernoui?"

"No." He glanced at her from over his shoulder, continuing to move about the small space, never letting his attention linger on her form. "They are days of rest for my people. We live in the woods. We hunt; we forage. We are constantly working with and against nature, so we built in time to rest."

"That's what Timresiet and Samseiet and Parlquoet are for."

"In your culture, yes. Not in mine."

"You do not have weekly days of rest."

"It is not so much to work thirty days of each month when three are meant for our ease."

"You make me feel lazy."

She smiled when he turned to face her, shadows keeping his face in darkness, his expression from her eyes. "I've seen you on Samseiet, my Prince. You don't take days off either."

"I'm a prince."

There was no joy in accepting the title.

"Even princes need to rest."

His arms spread wide, fingers grazing the smooth wood of the paneling. The gray of his eyes shadowed for a moment as he leaned against the wall, breathed in the moist air. "That's why I come here, fair Captain. No one ever seeks me here."

She stood carefully, testing her balance before she stepped away from the bed, rounded the wooden table to stand before him where he leaned in the corner. The slice in his shirt was shallow, the barbs of the whip having cut his skin, true enough, ripped the shirt, yes, but not done much damage beyond the surface. He would have a scar, but that was because of her magic. Had the wound been treated with tinctures and a wrap, likely nothing would have remained to tell the tale of tonight's adventure.

He didn't stop her from pressing the pads of her fingers to the mark, tracing the line from collar bone to the ridge of his sternum. "This is your sanctuary." She flattened her palm to his chest. "I did not mean to disturb it."

"You haven't."

Too far, always just an inch beyond a simple tilt of the head to press her lips to his, taste this prince who was far too pure and too honorable to be of the city she hated and yet was growing to care for because he lived within its walls.

"You're welcome here, Captain, if you need the space to retreat to."

Her rooms were her sanctuary, but that's not what he was offering her. If no one else could find him, she would know where to look. He gave her the key to his small place of peace, a place where he was alone, and she could be alone with him.

Poor man likely hadn't thought of all the implications of his offer.

Her smile dimmed with the realization, the want. "I would have us be friends, Kit."

He looked down at her, covered her hand on his chest, squeezed her fingers in a gentle caress. His pulse was steady beneath her touch, wonderfully alive against her, even as she knew his answer would be other than what she wished for. "I don't know that I have the strength to offer that, Eli."

Especially since friendship was not what she longed for, not what he longed for.

He'd offered more once, and she'd denied him.

"Please."

A final squeeze before he gently pushed her away, creating space between their bodies so he could brush around her, walk free.

She remained in her corner, eyes focused on the wall before her, unwilling to see whatever expression was on his face, if he would acquiesce or deny her request.

His footsteps paused at the door. "Ella."

She turned to him, her gaze carefully neutral so he would not see her hope or despair.

"I'll try."

He was gone before she could respond, the door closing at his back.

Her prince fled, and she wondered if she should give chase.

She looked at the glass window, knowing his rooms were only a story above her, easy enough to catch him if she chose.

But perhaps it was better to let him find her, be the one pursued rather than do the hunting.

After all, he'd never returned the shoe she'd lost that third night of the ball.

Find out what happens to Eli and Kit in the next installment of
the Never Lands Saga:

The Captain
A *Charming* Book Two

Appendix 1
The Lands of Shcew

It is quite the thing to close your eyes and wake in another time, in another place, in another land so very unlike your own that it is both wonderful and terrifying in turn.

Herein lies that which I have learned so far on my journeys to the Never Lands. Though I've yet to learn a great deal of the lands themselves, what I have been able to piece together is fascinating. From Kingdoms of giants to dead islands burned clean with dragon fire, the Lands are captivating.

I suppose, to begin, it would be appropriate to start with the planet's name. As you can imagine, a land so unlike our own and yet infinitely similar could rightly be called "Earth." In truth, they term the ground they walk on as such, but the planet itself has quite a different appellation.

Shcew.

Shcew received its name from the first bird that landed on the lands. There is a complicated history to which I was not privy. The basics of the story that I heard was that after the initial land masses formed, the world was dormant of life, waiting to be inhabited. The gods who created the planet, though this may well be only one creation story of the land, waited and watched and finally, from out of the dark wastes of their universe, a tiny bird, the closest approximation I can think of would be our sparrow, slipped through the atmosphere and settled on a small piece of earth at the top of their planet, laid its head upon the ground, and slept. It spread its wings wide, and sprawled its legs out, and from its body sprang the land of Prutwl, the great crown at the head of their world.

But that was only one myth, and who is to say if it is true or not?

The planet itself consists of six land masses. Some historians divide the southernmost continent into two distinct continents, but once upon a time, the lands were connected by a bridge and were as one.

Below is a brief history of each mass as I've learned so far. Most of my time has been spent in Lornai, predominantly in Spinick itself, so please forgive any misrepresentations as I've not the skills of a natural historian or geographer and have done the best I could.

Prutwl

The northernmost continent consists of a string of peninsulas circled together, vaguely resembling a large crown that might once have been worn by the world. Covered in snow and ice for twelve of the nineteen month year, Prutwl is home to the first races, those born of the elements when Shcew was created in the cosmos.

Though it is home to the elements, the land itself is bereft of magic, its people resenting the unnatural aspects of their brethren from other lands.

There is speculation that the animosity between magic and non-magic folk began when select rogue priests demanded sacrifice from the people of Prutwl, and rather than allowing their sons and daughters to be killed, the, for lack of a better word, ordinary folk rose up and forced the wizards and witches and false-gods, from the land and have kept it bereft of magic since. Those who possess even the slightest of magical talents are exiled, if not worse, according to legend.

Kirbi

It is known as a desert continent riddled with hidden oases of lush rain forests and barren subterranean villages. Most of the inhabitants live beneath the sands and rarely walk aboveground. Those who do make their homes in the rain forests battle Manticore and Yateveo for supremacy (again, the closest approximation of their terminology as based from our own linguistics and cultures). The Djinn are a hidden race, building their habitats deep within the jungles, concealed by the trees. The few trading ports on the outskirts of the continent discourage explorers though the riches found in the land tempt foreigners to overstay their welcome.

Zephra

Known as the vanishing isle, Zephra was once the most lush and beautiful of all the Never Lands. During the Third Age, the great dragons who made the island their home were betrayed by the humans who shared the island with them, the Miestians. The War of the Dragons raged for nearly fifteen hundred years before the dragons, fearing defeat, set the entire island on fire, killing all the inhabitants, flora, fauna, and human alike. With the destruction of the island, the dragons were said to have sunk into the ash of their homeland and fallen asleep, waiting for the next attack to come against them.

The island itself is thought to be more myth than truth as it is an untethered land mass and moves with the tides through the oceans. Those who see the island rarely live long enough to report back to anyone on its whereabouts, and its name is spoken in hushed whispers, as legend says that simply stringing the syllables together will call down the fiery wrath of the serpents who sleep there.

Wen

A series of island connected by bridges makes up the continent of Wen. The bridges were built by the first races as each of the five islands is the home of the elements of Shcew. Yes, there is a separate creation myth that lends strength to the assertion, just as Prutwl alleges the same. I shall endeavor to discover more of the truth as my travels allow.

The largest of the islands, Eao, is said to be the birthplace of earth and the birthplace of man. *Arising from the dust, man was made from water and air and given legs to walk and arms to build*, or so goes the ancient myth. I'Che is the land of water. Sool dedicates its soil to the breath of air that wraps around its great mountain. Lars is the furthest south of the equator and, as the hottest island in the chain, is a celebrant of fire. Roa Shar holds the great temple of Shcew and worships the Light that bathes the world, and the Dark that shelters it in slumber. It is dedicated to spirit, and learning to be one with the body and the earth.

Istar Ahn and Ohn

Twin continents at the southern pole, the lands were once connected by a strip of land called the Vein. When the bridge was destroyed, the lands separated into different entities in entirety. Istar refuses to allow visitors to their shores and trading was embargoed during the Second Golden Age.

Lornai

As the second largest continent on the planet, Lornai was once one nation but the *First Dragon War* saw the land split into nine independent kingdoms. Though small skirmishes still occur, the land is at general peace with the Northern Kingdoms of Drewes, Quifol, and Faoust bordered by mountains and the Middle Kingdoms separated by the Great Forest of Dienobo and its elven protectors, the Dienobolos. The Southern Kingdom of Spinick, the Great Walled City, was once the capital of the land, and still boasts the greatest resources on the continent.

The elves of course dispute this, but communication with them is limited at best.

At the end of the Great Dragon War, the Gods foretold that a son would be born to the King of the City during the rise of the Fourth Age and with his birth, the Land would either rise above itself or it would fall into the oceans. The full prophecy was lost long ago, though theories run rampant as to its origin throughout the kingdoms.

Appendix 2
The Calendar of the Never Lands

The planet of Shcew rotates on a thirty-two hour cycle. As with our world, they revolve around a sun at the center of their solar system. Because of their sun's enormity, and their relative size and rotational speed, one solar year for the planet lasts six hundred and twenty days. A leap year occurs every seven cycles, increasing the length of the year to six hundred and twenty two days.

The year is divided into nineteen months with eight day weeks. In opposition to our own yearly cycle, their New Year begins in the middle of their Summer. Though the day changes yearly, the month of V'Roshar hosts the Longest Day, a celebration of the Light of the World. As is custom, the Longest Day is a day of festival where upon great parties are held and torches are lit throughout the night to keep the sun shining for the whole thirty-two hours.

In contrast, Rashel, the mid-winter month, celebrates the Day of Night, the longest night of the year. A more sober celebration, the Worshippers of the Darkness hold silent vigils on this Night, fare-welling their dead, adjudicating grave crimes, remembering that from the dark we came and to the dark we must return. For others outside of the Darkness, the day is for family, often commencing with great parties that last until the dawn of the next morning.

The days of the week are as follows:

The First Day of the week is a day of rest on the continent of Lornai. Though the world follows the same structural month and date pattern, cultures change what each day is representative of. For example, in Kirbi, Timresiet is a day of religion. Vendors close down their shops and are expected to present themselves at their known houses of worship. Kirbi is a rather religious continent, as they have little else to unify them with. (It is another reason outsiders are mistrusted and denied entry into the land.) In Lornai, Spinick specifically, Timresiet is a day typified as a bathing day. Public bath houses open early and close late so that men and women can make use of the provided water to bathe in. Though other shops and stalls are open on this day, it is considered a day of light work and general rest.

Seventh and Eighth days are also days of rest, though many people choose to work on Parlquoet, Eighth Day, so as to prepare for the upcoming week. Parlquoet is also a day of religion in Lornai, though customs vary by kingdom.

Second through Sixth days are work days. The typical vendor opens his or her shop an hour after sunrise. The hour before is for setting up stalls since, at least in Spinick, the streets are required to be cleared on Timresiet as and per royal decree. Vendors are allowed to remain at their store fronts and shops until an hour after sunset, the curfew in place for their and their monarchy's protection. Outside of the city proper, such strict protocol is not enforced, though towns are subject to their own laws and guidelines.

In contrast to Spinick, the Dienobolos observe no weekly rest days, all eight spent working at something or another. They do, however, celebrate the Dark of the Moon as a three day stretch of the month wherein obligations are foregone for relaxation and meditation.

First Day:	Timresiet
Second Day:	Onoui
Third Day:	Vernoui
Fourth Day:	Saioui
Fifth Day:	Oweloui
Sixth Day:	Moui
Seventh Day:	Samseiet
Eighth Day:	Parlquoet

Appendix 3
A Closer Look at <u>Lornai</u>

The Elves of the **Dienobo** were the first settlers of the land. As an immortal race, they knew the importance of ensuring the wellbeing of their homeland. They cultivated the earth, nurtured the trees, found ways to coexist within the forests that once covered the continent proper. It was not until after the *First Dragon War* that the Dienobolos took up swords to defend their homes. By then, most of the continent had been conquered, the land stripped of forests, barren but for what was required to feed and build for the people. The elves, because of their hate for the destruction of their region, became warriors unparalleled among the races of the land. It was during the *Third Age* that they were relegated to their small remaining forested home. Upon threat of fire, ultimate destruction of all they knew, the Night Folk retreated to their forests, swearing peace unless their homes were invaded and then swift vengeance upon those who would dare their retribution.

Of **Traimktor** little is known even with their close proximity to the woods of the Dienobo. Rumor has it that the inhabitants of the Forbidden Realm were once elves. Beyond that truth, suspicion only. Some say that the men and women of Traimktor were so disgusted with the people of the land, their own kind included, they fled to the small kingdom and refused to leave for any reason, no contact with the world outside their own community. Even the elves that were once kin were forbidden the stolen land. Another myth is that the inhabitants of the small country were once elves, cursed to live alone, too violent even for the warriors of the wood to control. They were cursed to live like beasts as penance for the lives they had taken during the wars, cursed until they relearned their humanity.

Whether they are immortal as their brethren or short lived like the beastly forms they inhabit, it is unknown. But on quiet nights, if you listen carefully, you can hear the call of the wolves and the bears, griffin and wyvern deep within the trees.

During the first age, other races began to venture into the land. The once fertile lands of the south grew fallow, only the harshest, sturdiest of vegetation surviving as their caretakers failed to upkeep the earth. The Men of *Quifol* were a solitary people, a warring people. They held to the southern tip of the land, fighting back invaders though they seldom ventured past their own borders despite their deadly tendencies. Most of what is known of their land is speculation. The kings, leaders, of the grassland folk do not engage in trade among the other lands of their continent. They are considered a closed territory. Some say that there was a time when the Men of cQuic did leave their grasslands. Stories of young daughters going missing from playing in the fields, little misses disappearing from their beds at night, run rampant along the border of the land. The last story was told long ago, but Quifol's neighbors lock their doors at night, place totems outside their houses to keep the foreign men from their children.

Trolls do not take kindly to the abduction of their kin, male or female. As a mortal race, their lives ranging less than one hundred years, their children are their only source of immortality to them. The Faoustians fight hard to keep their land and families safe. Amusingly, as a short lived race, they do not fear death or battle, often plying their trade as swords for hire. Then again, when they are surrounded on all sides by battle hardened countries like Quifol and Gouldaria, the citizens of *Faoust* require hardy sword arms to protect themselves.

Following accordingly then, *Gouldaria* separates Drewes and Faoust. The dwarves, vicious, ruthless creatures that they are, are limited in the land they can conquer by the mountains that surround them and the fierce nations at their sides. Despite their bloodthirsty tendencies, the dwarves, as well as being trained soldiers, are skilled craftsmen and armorers. Perhaps their greatest despondency comes from sitting before their forges creating great weapons to cull their enemies with, and their enemies too far away to attack.

Thankfully, the mountains keep the dwarves from *Drewes*. Though the giants are a larger race, as mortal as their dwarfish neighbors, they are a gentle people. They are slow to anger, and slower still to war. Understandably, no nation wishes to provoke the large folk, though they've shown no tendency towards brutality throughout their long tenure as caretakers of the mountains.

Of *Mrgloth* there is nothing known. The land is steeped in magic but who can say aught else? The sand that blows from the desert is heavy with gold. Beyond that, nothing. All who have tried to breach their borders have died, bodies found broken and bloody, thrown to the rocks before ever reaching what lies beyond the giant hills. The first to forge a path to the nation will be hailed a hero, or die unheard from again.

Thankfully, the dragon shifters of *Arqueania* are a more tractable group. They trade openly, magic freely, live peacefully with their neighboring lands. Though fire runs rampant through their veins, making their dispositions quick and dangerous to displeasure, the men and women themselves are quite amiable, though a sadness lurks beneath their smiles. Whether they miss their kin from Zephra, or are kin at all, is unclear. But they've proven wise counsel and fair judges, swift to action and equally swift to penance when it is required. Then again, for a species that lives near unto five thousand years, many arguments could occur throughout a lifetime, and when tempers are so volatile, apologizing is a skill best learned young.

What, then, can be said of the humans? Of all the races of the lands, the residents of *Spinick*, the Great Walled city, are, perhaps, the least impressive of the lot. Engineers, pioneers, bastards and kings, the populace is a strange hodgepodge of the best and worst of the peoples of Lornai. Their first ruler was elected to the position. His kin have reigned justly ever since. They are the sons and daughters of the Gods, favored to be called the Heavenly Hosts children though little truth in the saying remains. Still, they must be blessed by some higher power, for they have never failed a test, always rose to a challenge, have defeated all and sundry sent against them and reigned as the mightiest of the kingdoms of Lornai though they are one of the smaller lands. Immortals too, magical, in part, the humans of Spinick are a mystery that is accepted as normal and unquestioned by the world.

Appendix 4
The Religions of Lornai

Dienobo: Worshippers of the Darkness

Since the beginning of time, there has been Darkness. From the ethos, came a great clap and into that Darkness was born life. Life grew and formed there, and with it there was peace. But light intruded, touched the children of the Night and bathed the ground they walked upon in brilliance, opening their eyes to a world unseen beneath a blanket of Ebony.

The Darkness allowed the light to shine, for even though the heavens were bright, they fell to Shadow in the end.

From the Night stepped forth aspects of the dark.

Pirie, the Lord of the Lit Path, the Master of the Void. To Pirie all prayers are heard and from Pirie all prayers are answered. The Priests of the Darkness were given the grave task of creating law for those who took solace in Shadow.

The *Liaea*, the Inner Blackness of the Body, that which is Born from the Dark Womb and Returns to the Ebony Grave. Healers, teachers, those who dedicated themselves to the welfare of others kneel before the Body of Night given name.

The Master of the Final Midnight, *Echi*, the Lord of Death, the Father of New Life. One cannot come without the Other. Judge and jury, the dedicants of Echi grant mercy, ensure repayment of the debt, protect the Shadows even unto the Blackness of their own souls.

Rouchim of the Earth, the Keeper of Secrets, the Lady of the Hallow Ground and Sacred Tree. They who till the earth, work within the dirt, wander the paths between trees, tread where four and two footed brethren run, worship all those creatures living under the Night's Same Sky and offer thanks to the Darkness for the gifts grown in black places pay homage to the Dark Mistress.

Ashet, the Laborer, the Sentinel, the Lord of the Forge. Those who worship the art of life, from crafting shelters to guarding the dreams of their people, to building boats to cross the waters that reflect back the light of the stars shining from the Void, give their love to the Lord who levels and remakes the world.

The Worshippers of the Darkness bear an affinity for the earth and all its natural creations. They draw strength and magic from the Night itself, walk dreams and darkened pathways too shadowed to invite others onto the road to new life.

Children of the Gods

Herein worship to the Gods.

Look to them for your Salvation.

Surprisingly, the polytheistic religion of Schew trends towards our traditional understanding of Greek Mythology with a hierarchy of gods to whom one should pray depending on circumstances. The general belief is that each person can associate with one or two of the primary gods whom they offer sacrifices to as their personal totems, honoring all the gods as a whole but with emphasis on their personal choices.

Like the Dienobolos, the religion is separated by aspect. For instance, *Atha* is the Goddess of Warfare and Justice, much like what the Greek Athena would have been known for. She also combines the religious beliefs of Artemis and Aphrodite as the patron Goddess for young women in love, the hunters and warriors, soldiers, and judges throughout the land.

Sei is representative of the natural world, both land and sea. He is as much the patron of the sailor as he is the farmer. Compared to our mythological references, he could be considered an amalgamation of Poseidon, Demeter, and Hephaestus. Considered a god of creation, he is given right of rule over craftsmen and artists as well.

Zeus, contrary to our foundation in myth, is a minor god of nature, in particular of the animals that run and fly. As a shape changing colossus, farmers, whose trade is in livestock, worship him. With sacrifice, it is said that Zeus will descend to the earthly plane of existence and seed both mare and heifer, increasing the quality of the livestock with his heavenly offspring.

The mightiest of the gods then is *Hades*, known as the Lord of Life. With the power over both the living and the dead, Hades rules the other gods of the pantheon, both as father and judge for all those under his care. Similar to our mythos, Hell remains a place of damnation of the spirit though they have no concept of "heaven" as we understand it. Since the Children of the Gods are mostly those of the immortal races, when Death does come for them, they are seeking the oblivion of the void rather than resurrection or continued existence elsewhere. Hell then is where those sentenced to "live on" go to suffer, complete with fire and brimstone.

End Notes:

The Gods are more myth than actual evidence to the people who worship them. Never having walked on the lands of Shcew, the gods are a distant faith to believe in. Since there is no origin story associated with the mythology, and since I seemed familiar enough with the religion itself, I speculate that I am not the first to cross from our world to theirs, and, as humans are like to do, those ancestors of mine who made the transition brought with them their own faiths and beliefs which were then incorporated within the world they lived in.

I should mention that, as a newer religion in the scheme of Shcew, the Gods are widely popular amongst evolving races as something to strive towards, as well as being looked down upon by other religions, such as the Dienobo, who discredit the beliefs of anyone else. To be fair, discredit is the incorrect term. The Dienobo are quite willing to believe that there are beings powerful enough to interact with the world on a creational basis, with the understanding that these beings are minor "gods" compared to the Darkness whom they worship.

As I have yet to explore more of the world than my brief stay has allowed, I expect I will be supplementing my appendices as I gain more information, so please bear with me as I go along.

Appendix 5
A Brief Pronunciation Guide

For simplicity's sake, I have used the Common Tongue of Lornai as the basis of pronunciation for the days of the week and months of the year below. The Dienobolos have a language of their own which I have done my best to spell phonetically throughout the narrative. Only basic translations exist of their tongue.

WORD	IPA PRONUNCIATION	PHONETIC PRONUNCIATION
BASIC PRONUNCIATION GUIDE: COMMON TONGUE OF LORNAI		
Months of the Year		
V'Roshar	vr - ouʃ - ɑːr	**vr**oom-**oce**an-**shar**d
Tippum	taɪp - ɛm	**type**-vell**um**
Dellum	diːl - ɛm	**deal**- vell**um**
Genlum	dʒen - lɛm	**gen**tle- vell**um**
Brumm	bruːm	**broom**
Yyxum	jaɪks - ɛm	**yikes**- vell**um**
Yuaar	hɪə(r)	**you-are**
Neise	Nis	**niece**
Quaar	kweɪ - ər	**quake-are**
Rashel	retʃəl	**rate-shell**
Pereshel	perɪ -ʃəl	**peri**sh-**shell**
Mishel	mɪt -ʃəl	**michelle**
Apshel	eɪp -ʃəl	**ape-shell**
Frenshel	friːn -ʃəl	**f-preen-shell**
Harshel	hær -ʃəl	**hair-shell**
Cresch	kræ –sch	**cra**sh-**shell**
Wipshel	waɪp -ʃəl	**wipe-shell**

Linkshel	lɪŋk -ʃəl	**link**-**shell**
Vellim	vel -iːm	**v**-f**ell**-s**eem**

Days of the Week		
First Day: Timresiet	taɪm riː'sɪt	**Time**-**reset**
Second Day: Onoui	ɑːn wiː	**on**-**Oui**ja
Third Day: Vernoui	vər'n wiː	**vern**acular-**Oui**ja
Fourth Day: Saioui	saɪ wiː	**sigh**-**Oui**ja
Fifth Day: Oweloui	aʊl wiː	**owl**-**Oui**ja
Sixth Day: Moui	em wiː	**m**-**Oui**ja
Seventh Day: Samseiet	sʌ'm siː ɪt	**sam**-**si**ght-**et**
Eighth Day: Parlquoet	pɑːlə - kwə ɪt	**parl**iament-**quo**te-**et**

The Never Lands		
Prutwl	pruː-tuːl	**pru**dence-**tulle**
Kirbi	kɜːrb-biː	**Curb**-**bee**
Zephra	z-ef-r-ɑː	**z**-**eff**-**r**-**ah**
Wen	wen	**when**
Lornai	lɔːr-naɪ	**lore**-**nigh**
Istar Ohn	ɪztɑːr oʊ-n	**Is**-**tar** **oh**m-n
Istar Ahn	ɪztɑːr ɑːn	**Is**-**tar** **khan**
Shcew	ʃuː	**shoe**

Lornai		
Dienobo	deɪ-ɪn-əʊbəʊ	**Dee**-en-**oboe**
Traimktor	treɪ-m-k-tɔːr	**trai**n-m-k-**tor**
Quifol	kwɑː'f- l	**coif**fure-waf**fle**

151

Faoust	faʊst	**faust**
Gouldaria	guːl-dæ(r)iə	**gulag-dahl(r)ia**
Drewes	druː es	**drew-s**
Mrgloth	mɜː(r)g-ləʊθ	**myrrh-g-loth**
Arqueania	ɑːk- keɪn- iə	**ark-cane-ia**
Spinick	spɪnɪk	**spinick**

Religions: Dienobo		
Dienobo	deɪ-ɪn-əʊbəʊ	**Dee-en-oboe**
Pirie	paɪ-riː	**pie-reach**
Liaea	laɪ-ə-ɑ	**Lie-a-ah**
Echi	eʃə	**echelon**
Rouchim	ruːeɪ-ʃəˈm	**roué-chemise**
Ashet	æʃ ɪt	**ash-et**

Religions: the Gods		
Atha	ɑːð- ɑː	**father-ah**
Sei	saɪ	**size**
Zeus	zuː es	**Zeus**
Hades	heɪdiːz	**Hades**

About the Author

Andi Lawrencovna lives in a small town in Northeast Ohio where she was born and raised. After completing her Masters in Creative Writing, she decided that it was time to let a little fantasy rule her life for a while. The Never Lands were born out of a frustration with happily-ever-afters, and a burning desire for the same.

For More Information on Andi and *The Never Lands,* visit her website at:

www.AndiLawrencovna.com